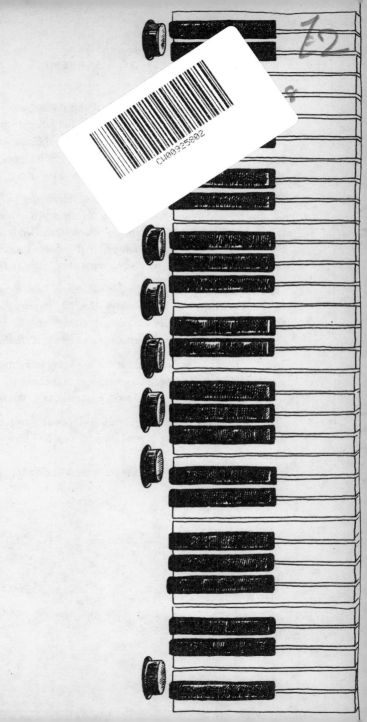

"The structure of this novel is original and deeply satisfying . . . The difficult thing to explain is why this mild, apparently artless tale should take you by the throat, why these threads, so insubstantial, should twist themselves into a bright filament, sturdy and enduring as fable"   ROSEMARY STOYLE, *Listener*

"A most impressive and original book, clear and yet full of depths . . . told in an almost biblical speech which apparently is true to the region's dialect, and to which Tom Geddes's translation gives complete authenticity, so that it doesn't sound like a translation at all"   ANTHONY THWAITE, *Sunday Telegraph*

"The Swedish author, of whom we will surely hear more, has a splendid translator in Tom Geddes. One has to remind oneself that the original dark story was not written in English"

VIRGINIA BARTON, *Catholic Herald*

"A short book, all the more powerful for being economical with words, and a gripping evocation of innocence and greed"

HELLE MICHELSEN, *Western Mail*

"Simply and directly told, this story is impossible to put down. Easily read at one sitting, it establishes a stark and bare world of biblical simplicity and power"

KEITH RUSSELL, *Newcastle Herald (Australia)*

TORGNY LINDGREN was born in Norsjö, Sweden, in 1938. He is the prize-winning author of novels, poems and short stories. His works so far published in English include his novels, *Bathsheba*, *Light* and *In Praise of Truth*, and a collection of stories, *Merab's Beauty*. His work is now translated into twenty-five languages.

TOM GEDDES has regularly been Torgny Lindgren's English translator. His translation of *The Way of a Serpent* was awarded the Bernard Shaw Anglo-Swedish translation prize.

Also by Torgny Lindgren in English translation

BATHSHEBA
MERAB'S BEAUTY
LIGHT
IN PRAISE OF TRUTH

Torgny Lindgren

THE WAY OF
A SERPENT

Translated from the Swedish
by Tom Geddes

THE HARVILL PRESS
LONDON

First published in Sweden with the title *Ormens Väg På Halleberget*
by P.A. Norstedt & Söners, Stockholm, 1982

First published in Great Britain in 1990 by Collins Harvill

This paperback edition first published in 1997 by
The Harvill Press, 84 Thornhill Road, London N1 1RD

2 4 6 8 10 9 7 5 3 1

© Torgny Lindgren, 1982
English translation © Harvill, 1990

Torgny Lindgren asserts the moral right to be identified as the author of this work

A CIP catalogue record for this book is available from the British Library

ISBN 1 86046 261 8

Photoset in Linotron Ehrhardt by Rowlands Phototypesetting Ltd

Printed and bound in Great Britain by Mackays of Chatham

Half title illustration: Newell and Sorrell,
with the Victorian Reed Organ and Harmonium Museum

THE WAY OF
A SERPENT

Appendix to the Secretary's Annual Report to the Västerbotten County Agricultural Society, 1882

In the course of my journey along the valley of the Vindel River in October last I devoted one day to visiting the place close to the boundary between the parishes of Lycksele and Norsjö known as Slough Hill, where a minor natural disaster is said to have occurred in the middle of the last decade. A young woman, Tilda Markström, who runs the local village shop, guided me to the spot. She maintained that her father, Karl Markström, a shopkeeper, had perished there in a landslide. To what extent this accords with the truth is, however, a matter on which I will not speculate. The inhabitants of these godforsaken backwoods have an unfortunate tendency to prefer stories to actual reality; these people lack all understanding of scientific principles.

That a landslide or landslip has occurred here would nevertheless seem to be indisputable. The escarpment of the landslide has a length of some 300 ells, the collapsed mass of soil, predominantly composed of boulders and moraine gravel, seems to have largely disappeared into the marsh that lies below the escarpment. No trace of habitations etc. is to be observed, but the higher ground would appear to have been cultivated from time to time.

The local populace do not seem to have made any significant

observations; they do not recall any fissuring, subsidence, etc. which might be consistent with the event, they appear simply to believe that God's creation and transformation of the world goes on continuously. Creation is (according to them) an unending process.

The place has acquired the name "New Hollow". The word "hollow" in this part of the country signifies a depression or valley of not very considerable extent. Its location is marked on the attached map with the symbol †.

Umeå, 11th December, 1882.
Rutger Bygdelius
Secretary to the Västerbotten County Agricultural Society

[I]

O Lord, was it him, Karl Orsa the farmer and shopkeeper, you wanted to bury that time when you tore apart Slough Hill like that, or was it me and my house and Johanna? And the children who had not yet lived their lives?

It doesn't happen in these parts, they say. Earthquakes, chasms, upheavals. Never.

That is all I want to ask.

You know my circumstances.

The language I am speaking to you in, O Lord, I learned at Baggböle, from Jacob.

"Circumstances" is a grand word.

I will tell you the whole story, Lord, I will tell you the whole story from beginning to end, and then I will ask you about the things that I do not understand.

Johan Johansson is my name, called Bragging Johnny by the folks around here – and probably known by that name even to you, who make no distinctions between people – born at Slough Hill in 1849, the year that my mother's father, Alexis, hanged himself in one of Ol Karlsa's pine trees – he had no forest of his own left by then – and the same year that two of Johan Olov's bulls drowned in the spring near Farm Marsh and so gave it its name, the Ox Spring – because everything has to have a name.

If you, Lord, ever need a scoop of water that will quench the thirst of an eternal being, then I advise you to go to the Ox Spring. It's as clear and cold as the air between the stars and it's just ten paces from the last footbridge before Fir Hill.

You know that I was born defiant, you created me defiant. And you've always spoken to me and said: Do not be defiant, Bragging Johnny. You are strange like that, you form us in a very particular way, boastful or pig-headed or whatever, and then you use up our lives telling us that is exactly what we should not be, we're not to be the particular way you created us.

But on the other hand, you were fair in not giving me very much to vent my defiance on. If you'd made me the son of a shopkeeper or a big farmer then I might have become a dangerous man with all that stubbornness and obstinacy built into me, I could have been a difficult master; but in the circumstances you put me in my defiance was so slight and ineffectual that it seemed no more than a wasting disease within me. Lord, to whom shall we go?

It's almost like an abyss you made here at Slough Hill, and as I'm sitting now my legs hang down over the chasm, I don't feel any fear, after what happened I can hang my legs over any precipice, I know that you can open up abysses wherever and whenever you fancy, and even here above the abyss – or whatever this great hole ought to be called – I can feel defiance within me. He restoreth my soul, he leadeth me in the paths of righteousness for his name's sake.

No, you let me be born without any father at all, and that was probably just as well, we'd have had to find food for him too – you gave me indifference at birth to water down the defiance with – and he can't have been much of a man, because you took him to the asylum at Pitholmen and there he just faded away and died.

But in his stead we did have this harmonium that Rönn, mother's godfather, the carpenter from Tjöln, had built for her and that sometimes earned us a crust of bread with its flighty tunes, especially if you pulled out the stops called Principal and Flute.

And one of them shall not fall on the ground without your Father. But the very hairs of your head are all numbered.

They used to fetch mother on Saturday evenings when she'd done the milking, they'd be raucous and merry, they would carry out the harmonium and put it on a flat wagon or a sledge, and put mother, who was part and parcel of their fun, next to the driver, and then they'd drive off to some outhouse or kitchen or barn and there they would dance right through to morning milking, and we used to be woken up when they lifted the harmonium down at the front door steps and when mother clattered the rings on the stove.

He didn't have any forest of his own, my grandfather, nor any upland plots or meadow, not a scrap did he have, although he wasn't born without any. But he wasted the whole lot, the sedge meadow and the ploughland, Meadow Hill and the Rock-lands. And when he'd lost everything he fell into poverty and want.

Yet he was as innocent as a newborn babe, he didn't drink spirits, he just frittered away his property like a little child walking about on the grass scattering behind him whatever he had in his hands. He was easy-going and good-natured and careless, he made his deals with Ol Karlsa – you have to do business, he would say – there were horseshoes and horseshoe nails and axes and saw-blades and salt and sugar and iron for the smithy and weaving reeds for grandmother.

He had no money, but things could always be pawned or mortgaged. Ol Karlsa had printed bonds all ready. The plough-land and Meadow Hill and the sedge meadow and the Rocklands, and another day, and tomorrow – yes, precisely: another day and a tomorrow would come when he would have to repay these small sums with interest. But the year before I was born, Lord, you let Ol Karlsa come along with the bonds, carrying them in Bible covers from which he'd removed the Word of God and put in all his own papers tied with leather straps. It was a Sunday, and grandfather said that it made him glad to see a shopkeeper who observed the day of rest with such grace and devotion that he carried the Word with him under his arm wherever he went.

"You're a mighty pious shopkeeper," he said.

Shopkeeper is what grandfather said, though Ol Karlsa was really an ordinary farmer like himself, it was only through loan-sharking that he'd started dealing in all kinds of goods and had become a kind of trader. And why, Lord, did you set farmers to rule this glorious earth that you created and why did you fill them with wickedness and low cunning and lust for power so they aren't like human beings at all?

"It's the bonds," said Ol Karlsa. "I've had the Word of the Lord rebound in ox-hide."

"Ah," said grandfather, "it's the bonds you're out walking with."

And he went on innocently: "Mother could give us a drop of beer if we go inside, it's a week old and just at its best."

But Ol Karlsa put on a show of reluctance, he'd drunk at the spring by Fir Hill and on Sundays he wouldn't touch beer if it was fermented, and it was cash he was after right now, and it was marvellous how well the barley was coming on here on the hillside, but it must be the sun and the lack of wind.

"But we can sit ourselves down, anyway," said grandfather.

When he was sitting Ol Karlsa said: "Aye. These bonds."

"I haven't any cash," said grandfather. "I'll have some by and by."

"I'm going into Skellefteå tomorrow," said Ol Karlsa. "I'll be taking the bonds with me."

"I think you're right about the barley," said grandfather. "Always in the lee and plenty of sun."

But by and by, he said, by and by he would clear the land behind the byre, another patch of barley, and he would dig a ditch right down the hillside and a bit into the marsh and there he could have a hayfield and some grazing; he'd warrant that by and by crops and cash, and calves and kids and lambs and skins and God's mercy and blessing . . .

But Ol Karlsa wouldn't accept by and by, he even had an almanac with him and that just had names of days and months, but not by and by. Debt-recovery proceedings and courts and registration of title had their months and days and to every thing there is a reason, and a time to every purpose under the heaven. A time to plant and a time to pluck up that which is planted. A time to kill, and a time to heal, a time to break down, and a time to build up. A time to weep, a time to laugh. And a time to mourn. But for by and by? There's none for by and by.

"Why didn't you kill him?" grandmother said afterwards.

"It didn't occur to me," said grandfather.

She thought of the strength he had in him and you know it too: he had performed miracles, carried a hundredweight sack on his outstretched arms, stood under the belly of a mare and heaved her up, lifted two fully-grown men on the palms of his hands, straightened out a number nine horseshoe – though no one knows if there were any such shire-horses here in those days.

"But why didn't you kill him?" said grandmother.

"That just wasn't the way it went," said grandfather.

In the autumn, in October, after the threshing, in the middle of the shearing and before the days of baking the bread, Ol Karlsa arrived with the title deed.

"Crofter or freeholder," he said, "you'll always be the same, Alexis. And now I've got what is mine. And you've paid your way. Like a man. And I can buy the wool. And if you do have

13

any beer . . . And we can come to terms about the rent. And if I buy the wool it will be for cash. Cash for the rent."

"Rent?" said grandfather. "For my own place?"

"For my place," said Ol Karlsa and brought out the title deed. "We can come to terms, I'm sure. We've always come to terms.

"I'm not a wicked man," he added – but grandfather could see wickedness glinting in his eyes.

Why didn't he kill him, that's what I say to you, Lord, and you probably say the same thing: Why didn't he kill him! Ol Karlsa was sixty-one, grandfather getting on for fifty-seven, and Ol Karlsa's soul was bound in the bundle of life with the Lord, but grandfather's wasn't.

My mother, she was seventeen that autumn, she brought out the beer and they came to terms about the rent and grandfather said that the other children, Lina and Eva and Tilda and Maria and Alida, they had gone out into the world now and it was only she, Thea, who was left and she had this gift for music and the harmonium that Rönn from Tjöln had built for her, and she played a hymn.

"There'll always be a way to manage," said Ol Karlsa. "But you should have had a boy."

"That just wasn't the way it went," said grandfather. "She plays, and the others dance."

[II]

Let's start from the beginning.

About paying rent. Back in '49, the first autumn of my life, grandfather went over to Skellefteå with the mirror, his own wedding ring and grandmother's, and the porcelain cock grandmother had got as wages in service at Böle, and it was just enough.

But by the next year he couldn't see how to cope.

Dear Lord: paying rent!

One year, the year of mourning, was rent-free for those of us who were left, mother and grandmother and myself, and I had just learned to walk.

"I'm not an evil man," said Ol Karlsa. "This year I'll let you have it gratis and for nothing. As ye have freely received, so shall ye also freely give."

But the next autumn mother had to find it all herself. She was twenty then.

"Where would we get the money from?" mother asked.

But Ol Karlsa just leered at her, you know how he used to leer. He took out his watch and leered at her as if the time had something to do with the rent. It was the middle of the day, and he leered at grandmother and me and then at mother again.

"What's his name?" he said.

"Johan," said mother. "After his dad's father."

"So he has a grandfather on his father's side," said Ol Karlsa.

"Of course he has," said grandmother. "A grandfather. Of course he has."

He grew fat in his last few years, did Ol Karlsa. He wanted to possess everything, even that: rolls of fat on his neck, bags of lard under his eyes, lumps of tallow on his fingers, blobs of fat everywhere – he should lack nothing.

"Money," he said. "I have that already. Enough and to spare."

That was a strange thing to say. It was the first time in his life that he'd said it. He was getting at something.

Unto everyone that hath shall be given, and he shall have abundance; but from him that hath not shall be taken away even that which he hath. It was quite clear what he was thinking.

"And firewood," he went on. "You two poor women and no man. No, there can't be any question of money."

If there was ever a time when you, Lord, should have intervened, it was then, that was the right moment for your providence, but nothing happened, nothing in particular. Grandmother prayed silently so hard that her whole face wrinkled up, and mother grabbed her hymn book and held it to her belly as if to protect herself. But Ol Karlsa sat down on the wood-bin and said:

"Won't you play for me, Thea?"

And that wasn't much to ask; music is a sort of comfort, and while you're playing it's as if you're given a respite from other things. She played hymns and pieces from *Songs of the Lamb* and he seemed to enjoy listening to them. He shut his eyes and waggled his shoes up and down – the farmers here have always been partial to music – and for a while grandmother thought he would be content with this and fall asleep.

But in the middle of "Out of the depths have I cried, O Lord. Lord, hear my voice: let thine ears be attentive to the voice of my supplications," he roused himself, got up, stepped across to mother and pushed in all the stops so that the harmonium suddenly fell silent, and he told grandmother to take the little boy, poor thing, and go outside, for now he was going to settle this matter of the rent and it would be quite enough if he just had Thea to settle the business with.

And you, Lord, who had also created Ol Karlsa, you know how he collected that rent, you weren't caught unawares by it. The fold-away bed was at the far end of the kitchen, and that's where he claimed his rights and we won't argue about those rights. He was as slow and long-winded and clumsy as an old boar and Lord, to whom shall we go?

At that time, on his first such visit, I was two, mother was twenty, Karl Orsa, his son, was twenty-eight and grandmother had only two years left.

Later in the autumn he came with two loads of birch-wood and half a sack of salt and a pair of shoes from Skellefteå for mother. Thou shalt by no means come out thence till thou hast paid the uttermost farthing, and mother paid our way, for we've never had any choice but to pay our way.

Karl Orsa, the son, he was different. He never said a word and he was tall and thin and kind of gloomy; he never joined in when they fetched the harmonium and mother, he never learned to dance, and why should he have danced, he had enough as it was, two and a half thousand acres of forest, fifty acres of ploughland, Hill Marsh and Long Marsh for hay, thirteen cows in the byre and two horses and the shop and he was going to have it all to himself, so he had no need to dance.

You can't see the bottom from up here on the edge, Lord, that's how deep this pit is that you made. It's called New Hollow, it was called New Hollow in the first year, everything has to have a name, and nobody knew afterwards who was the first to call it that.

When mother realised that she was in the family way, you,

Lord, put it into her mind to go to Ol Karlsa. He had running sores on one leg now and sat in the parlour behind the shop. It was the beginning of spring and there was muddy water pouring from mother's boots. She'd also had in mind to say that they, she and Ol Karlsa, had brought it on themselves to be expecting a littl'un together. She had a craving and was eating salt straight from the sack.

"Can't be true," he said, rubbing his leg. "I'm old and my hands are shaking. And now I've got leg sores."

And he mentioned his wife too: "Haven't even been near Magda these last two years," he said.

"Our Lord knows how this happened," said mother. "What you've got us into. It's because of the rent that you took."

"The rent?" he said.

"Yes, the rent," mother said.

"It's easy enough to see you're in the family way," he said. "And even if there's no father for the young 'un he does at least have a grandfather. Of course he has."

And mother had to defend herself:

"Johan does have a father. It's down in the parish register. But he fell ill. He was taken away to Pitholmen. The asylum."

"I'm in the process of handing things over," said Ol Karlsa. "I hand over a little bit each day. The forest. And the ploughland. And the shop. And the hay meadows."

"And you're handing over me and mine as well?"

"I'm handing over everything. When you have running sores you didn't ought to hold on to anything. Once you get leg sores you should step aside."

"And you're sure it's leg sores?" said mother.

"If it isn't something even worse," said Ol Karlsa. "But if it's the will of the Lord."

You know he always spoke like that.

"You'll have to come to an arrangement with my boy, Karl

Orsa. About the rent. I'm done with all that now," he said. "But he won't be unreasonable, I'm sure. Though of course . . . if it weren't for the leg sores . . . And you can take a sugar-loaf for your boy. Or two. Take two sugar-loaves."

His last few months were hard for Ol Karlsa, it was a kind of justice, the running sores spread up his legs and over his belly and chest and arms and head and he couldn't take his food any more. And he knew that the only thing to keep meat fresh is salt, so he got Magda to cover his sores with coarse salt every day, morning and evening. It was dreadfully painful at first and he screamed terribly, but gradually his flesh got used to the salt, and in his last few days the pain seemed to have stopped, but by then he was so far gone that it was no longer any comfort. Karl Orsa put the funeral off till Michaelmas, since the corpse was already salted anyway, he said, and it was a thundery summer when all the work seemed to take three times as long as usual.

My sister, my first sister, was born in the middle of summer, and she was called Eva after one of my mother's sisters. Mother seemed really glad to have her – you, Lord, understand these things better than I do – and she used to carry her to the meadows in the birch-bark sling on her back that grandfather had made while she was expecting me. She was light in colour like us, not dark like Ol Karlsa's family. "And I'll teach her to play," said mother, "I'll teach her to play light music."

[III]

"This was for you," said Karl Orsa when he came that autumn after taking over everything that Ol Karlsa had left him.

"It was probably made in Italy," he said. "Or Palestine. My old man started talking about it the last day his head was clear. 'I want Thea to have the mirror,' he said. 'As a sort of memento. I've always liked her music. The mirror with the snails and crystals and shellfish on the frame. The one I bought in Piteå when I sold the dog-skins to the Crown.'"

And mother just took the mirror and hung it on the nail that had been left there ever since her father had left with the old mirror.

"Leave the nail there," grandfather had said. "You never know."

Just as if he had sensed it: there will be another mirror one day.

"That's a fine-looking mirror, that is," said grandmother.

"What's her name?" said Karl Orsa, nodding in the direction of the baby girl.

"Eva," said mother. "After her aunt who went down to Umeå to go into service with a clergyman. She's in a place called Ön."

Did he realise that it was his own sister he was looking at? Mother could have said it, she should have said it, but she looked at the mirror and that just wasn't the way it went.

Lord, putting things into proper words is hard, how do you say at a loss?

"But the rent," mother said. "Did he remember to say anything about the rent at the end?"

"Only the mirror," said Karl Orsa. "He had already handed over the shop and the farm. Before he died it was mainly just little things that he still had to sort out. All that remained were unimportant little things and death."

He was thirty and a mature man, was Karl Orsa. He had dark brown hair with a slightly fairer fringe of beard that was always neatly trimmed, he stood stiff and straight, and he wore a frock coat and moved slowly, he would never do anything hastily or needlessly.

"I'll sit down and check the book after New Year," he said. "And we'll see about the rent then."

"So there was a book, then?" mother said.

"It's all written down," said Karl Orsa. "He was very particular, the old man. And for this year it's been paid up. He's written that down in the book."

"I was thinking more about by and by," said mother. "I'm on my own. And no money."

"If it weren't for the shop," said Karl Orsa. "But the shop can't be run without cash. Otherwise there'd be no need for money. But I have to have it for the shop."

And before leaving he added: "But you can always have credit. If you need it. It'll be all right."

On Boxing Day they came to fetch mother and the harmonium, to go dancing at Ristjöln, and she took Eva with her in the sling, she needed to be breast-fed.

She brought a fellow back home with her from Ristjöln. He came on skis behind the sleigh where mother and Eva sat in sheepskin rugs and behind the sledge carrying the harmonium. His name was Jacob and he had only one eye. And he was a

Southerner: he said himself that he came from the land of Canaan but it was probably no further than Ångermanland or at most Småland.

Lord, it was you that had sent him.

"He didn't dance," said mother. "He looked after the baby for me over at Ristjöln. Not a single dance."

He'd come to Umeå on a boat. He'd worked for a timber merchant there. He'd been a farm-hand at Sävar. And barked poles for hay-racks at Röbäck. And last autumn he'd been squaring timber at Burträsk. And now he'd come north with a carter. Grandmother asked about the eye but he didn't really explain it, he just held his hand over the empty eye socket and said he'd lost it but could see quite well with the one he still had, he didn't expect too much. He was a small, thin man with sloping shoulders, he had a quick and easy laugh, especially when he played with Eva, and on the very first day he arrived he carved me a toy man that could stand and rock on the edge of the table. He had hardly anything in his rucksack, just a plane and a rasp and knives and two chisels; no, he was nothing special, was Jacob, rather the opposite. He was just the man mother needed.

When Karl Orsa came over at Epiphany Jacob brought out a leather pouch straight away and paid the rent. For which of you, intending to build a tower, sitteth not down first, and counteth the cost, whether he have sufficient to finish it? Rejoice with me; for I have found the piece which I had lost!

"So some money has come into the house," said Karl Orsa. "Real big money."

And mother seemed neither to see nor hear, she went over to the harmonium and began to play, and Karl Orsa stood for a while as if he was embarrassed and confused. He should have said something more but that just wasn't the way it went. He put the money in his coat pocket and leered at mother, and she trod the pedals faster than usual and played "I neither gold nor wealth possess, My lot in life is humble, But I my heavenly Father bless, Though I on earth may stumble," and grandmother went up to this Jacob whom she hardly knew and stroked his cheek as if he was a little child, and it seemed as if the business of the rent was now finished with for good and all.

Seven years he stayed, did Jacob. He even bought a cow. He had wages outstanding at Burträsk and he went there and fetched a cow and paid a bit extra to make up the difference. It was a black cow and she was called Angel. He could do most things, he mended the shoes and made rakes and coffins for people and he squared timber for folks who were going to build, he made two lots of wood tar, and made the barrels himself, and he fished and nailed up pike to dry on the wall of the byre. But he couldn't hunt or shoot: it was his aiming eye that he'd lost. And mother had two girls by him, Rachel and Sarah. And he got himself two Lapland-dog bitches to breed, and they had eight pups altogether, and he kept them in an enclosure all winter so they turned wild, and in the spring he slaughtered them and prepared the skins and when autumn came he made a fur coat for mother, so that she wouldn't freeze to death when she travelled around with the harmonium, and dogskin gloves for her playing hands.

And he always made sure there was money to pay the rent with, he was careful about that, although it wasn't in his nature to be careful about anything, and he had a weakness for gin. He got it from Karl Orsa who brought it in casks from Skellefteå. Jacob would buy a jar at a time and then drink it until it was finished, which would take about three days, and afterwards he was like a little child, crying and sorrowful and wanting us to forgive him although he hadn't done anything evil, and mother had to play some *Songs of the Lamb* for him so that it sounded like a prayer-meeting, and it was strange that such a small man

23

could drink so heartily and call so loudly and powerfully to God.

Do you remember that I used to call him father?

"You can call Jacob father," said mother, "he deserves something for all his hard work, and we must try to give him some of the little we have so that he won't feel dissatisfied.

"We should always do what we can," she added.

So I called him father, though I only ever thought of him as Jacob.

Karl Orsa drank gin too. But not like Jacob so that he got drunk and sentimental and childish, just a small dram each day to stop his rigid body seizing up completely and to help him cope with speaking to people. He was so serious and sombre in his thoughts that it was hard for him to talk, and he never laughed except when he had to.

In the autumn of the first year that Jacob was with us grandmother fell ill, it was in her belly and caused her terrible pain, you Lord know what it was but we supposed it was cancer, and she couldn't take food and had to stay in bed for two months and just before Christmas she died. And it was mostly Jacob who looked after her, he seemed to be used to it in the same way that he seemed to be used to almost everything, it was he who lifted her up and bathed her back when it got sore and it was he who managed to keep her just alive with gruel and combed her hair and read her the Psalms and the Epistles to the Corinthians and when she was dead he washed her once more and it was he who made the coffin for her. We then that are strong ought to bear the infirmities of the weak, and not to please ourselves.

In the autumn of 1860, when I was eleven, mother was twenty-nine, Eva eight, Sarah five and Rachel three, they came to fetch Jacob. What the reason was they didn't say but it was something that had happened on the boat he'd come to Umeå on. It was thanks to Karl Orsa that they found him – he'd gone to a lot of trouble in Skellefteå, had Karl Orsa, to find out who

24

Jacob really was, and it turned out that they'd been looking for him all these years. The last thing he did at our place was to give mother the money for the next year's rent.

They took Jacob in the sleigh; the skis that he'd come on were left behind and so was Angel, the cow. The same evening Karl Orsa came and said that the fact was that Jacob was a thief, that he'd stolen money on that boat and before that he'd stolen a lot of things, thieving was part of his nature.

"But you're in credit," he told mother. "You haven't got a man now but I'll give you credit."

And mother, she paid the rent in advance for the next year and said that she hadn't known that he was a thief, he hadn't stolen anything at our place, no he'd given more than he'd taken, although there wasn't much to take of course, and that the only thing that mattered to her was just to do what she could.

"Can't you play a tune for me, Thea?" said Karl Orsa.

"No," said mother. "I'm still free of debt. But the day I owe you something, then I'll play for you. Then you'll have a right to the music. But not until then."

[IV]

In '62, just after New Year, Karl Orsa arrived. He came empty-handed except that he brought a sugar-loaf for Sarah and Rachel; he was in no hurry to broach his business, he wore his frock coat as if he was out for a Sunday walk.

I was thirteen, although I wasn't big, I'd been ditching over at Home-Farm Marsh all autumn and got food and a half farm-hand's wages and mother had been playing every weekend, she was turned thirty now and the harmonium had lost a stop and Rönn was dead so it wasn't repaired.

"We'll manage all right now," she said when I came home with the money.

That was typical of her: We'll manage all right now.

"Though we haven't paid the rent," she added. "If only the rent wasn't still due."

"He's been out to work," said Karl Orsa. "Your boy Johnny. Well now."

And mother brought out the money and laid it on the corner of the table and told him to count it, she hadn't been able to count this big pile herself. He could take what was owing for the rent, what was left over she'd use for all the other expenses and food and clothes and salt for the food and the bone buttons and salt herring that she'd taken on tick from his shop.

But he barely looked at the money, he leered at mother and

unbuttoned his coat and buttoned it up again and smoothed down his hair and fidgeted with his feet as if he was cold or needed to pee.

"Is that all your money?" he said. "That lot?"

"Don't you have the heart to take it, Karl Orsa?" mother said. "You needn't feel sorry for us. Right's right."

"I don't have to count it," he said. "I can see from here that it's not half the rent. And I won't take your last pennies. You keep 'em. I'm not an evil man."

"By and by," I said. "By and by I'll be going ditching again. And I'll dig another patch behind the byre. By and by. And maybe manage to afford a horse. And I might even get a tar-still. By and by."

But they didn't hear me, I was too small and weedy, my voice was too feeble, they didn't even look at me, mother didn't dare to.

Therefore I take pleasure in infirmities, in reproaches, in necessities, in persecutions, in distresses: for when I am weak, then am I strong.

"Angel," mother said. "Our cow. You can take her."

But Karl Orsa didn't say anything, it wasn't Angel he was after, nor the cash; but every man is tempted when he is drawn away of his own lust and enticed, it was mother he was after.

"A whole cow," said mother. "If that isn't enough I don't know what is."

But he made a show of reluctance, it was as if he had to be coaxed into accepting that cow.

"The hay will be gone by March anyway," said mother. "We're a bit short. And what are we to do then? You may as well take her. She'll only be a burden to us by spring."

And in the end he had to turn his attention to this damned cow.

"I suppose I'll have to go and take a look at her then," he said. "That's not to say . . . But since you insist, Thea."

27

And in the byre he pinched Angel hard, inspected her legs and ran his hand over her back.

"How old would she be?" he asked.

"She'll be ten this autumn," said mother.

"She's a bit thin and scraggy," said Karl Orsa.

And that was the truth, there was nothing special about our cow, Angel. An old cow, a bit down in the mouth and listless.

Lord, you knew Angel too. That's how it was.

And Karl Orsa examined her udder.

"Little sores on the teats," he said. "And the udder is empty."

Then he leered at mother, her bosom was full and firm. You could see he was thinking: those tits.

"What about for slaughter?" mother tried. "For butchering?"

Then he had to go over Angel with his hands and eyes again, he knew a thing or two about butcher's meat as well.

"She hasn't much meat on her," he said. "She's not much more than skin and bone. Like an empty hay-rick. Scrawny little beast."

And he made eyes at mother again and you could see he was thinking: flesh.

Mother's final suggestion was: "The skin? A cow-hide at least?"

But it didn't even seem worth considering: "Hides don't sell. Nobody's buying hides. Specially cow-hides. There's more hide than live animals. No point at all."

He made eyes at mother's skin too, she had bare arms and a bare neck and you could see he'd made his mind up how the rent was to be paid this year.

He would have the music, of course. Eva was ten now, she was the one who had to play, perhaps mother had spoken to her, and she played dance music and hymns and a tune that mother had made up herself, and it sounded sort of simpler and merrier from her than when mother played, and when she had finished playing the new tune Karl Orsa said: "I haven't heard that piece before. It was kind of sad even though it went fast."

"I made up that piece myself," mother said. "It's called 'Karl Orsa's Polka'."

Everything has to have a name, somebody says the name and that's how it stays, for whatsoever Adam called every living creature, that was the name thereof. "Karl Orsa's Polka".

And afterwards, when Eva had played till he'd had his fill of music, I took Eva and Sarah and Rachel with me out to the byre and we sat up close to Angel who at any rate was marvellously warm, and Eva said a poem that she had learned by heart, she was extraordinary when it came to learning things by heart: "Thou, whose heart divine did bleed, For the sake of souls untold, Thou who succours those in need And whose arms the babes unfold! Jesu! from all worldly cares By thy guidance I am freed, And my eyes with blissful tears Greet in thee a friend indeed. Why then do I yet despair And from secret torments smart? Danger, Lord! surrounds me here, Frail and helpless is my heart. Do not leave me, for this world Would me from thy love withdraw, From its vain foundations hurled Keep my faith for evermore. Make of woman's heart the shrine Where thy love most brightly burns, Let her feelings gently shine Where a mind uneasy turns. May her hands to those in pain Cups of solace kindly reach, In a world of strife and strain May she comfort bring to each."

Lord, to whom shall we go?

About Angel, while I remember it: she lived to sixteen. Then she got colic and had to be slaughtered and was buried hide and all, as we didn't know for sure.

I stood at the door of the byre and kept watch and saw him leave. It didn't show on him that he'd collected the rent, he didn't seem to be carrying anything, just the opposite: he was swinging his legs in an unusual way and waving his arms about almost as if it was he who'd paid out something and freed himself from debt.

And when we came in again mother was sitting at the harmonium. "Be not dismayed if brutal force High honour is accorded And those who show the least remorse So often are rewarded. For Death shall one day reap them all And they like grass to earth will fall And wither and be trampled."

And I found the glue pot that Jacob had put away under the floor of the byre, and glued back that stop on the harmonium, MELODIA.

[V]

Zuleima, who she was I don't know. Nobody knows anything, and I really have enquired, but no one, not even the parson. She has a cloth around her hair and something like a shawl over her shoulders and she's holding a tall narrow water-jug in front of her and her dress is white. She was on the first page of the almanac in '63.

Lord, do you know who Zuleima is?

Karl Orsa started with the almanacs in '63. He bought them in Skellefteå. On the second page after Zuleima it said that they cost fourteen öre and that it was Norstedts and Sons who had made them, he gave them to his biggest customers and his name was stamped on the cover and he gave them to mother as a kind of receipt.

If they'd put a head-cloth round mother's hair and dressed her in a white dress and a motley shawl and if they'd put her in the almanac she would have looked like Zuleima. What a handsome woman she was!

There is a Zuleima at Risliden, I've often heard people mention her, but she was born in '63 and must have been christened after the almanac.

For the first week, right across the whole week from New Year's Day to Epiphany, through Abel and Enoch and Titus and Simeon, he had carefully written "DEBT PAID" and then he had signed his own name on Augustus' day, when the moon was in the first quarter.

Mother wouldn't accept the almanac at first.

"What do I need it for?" she said. "I never read the almanac. And you're surely not giving it away for nothing? You must have something in mind, Karl Orsa."

"Not at all," he said. "But the children can have it to leaf through. And to look at the letters."

"I don't want to be guilty of more debt than I already am," said mother and tried to slip the almanac into his hand.

But he backed off towards the door and drew his hand away and said that it might well be that whosoever shall keep the whole law and yet offend in one point, he is guilty of all, and that no one was totally free of debt.

"So take the almanac and keep it, Thea," he said.

We must have had some fifteen almanacs altogether over the years, and we got used to the almanacs just the same as we got used to everything else, if we hadn't received them we'd probably have missed them – the last almanac is in my pocket, 1877 – and in all of them was written "DEBT PAID".

Jacob had taught me my letters and how to talk properly.

He wrote them with bits of charcoal on the wall of the byre, the second time he was with us he pulled the wall down and moved it a few feet and then the logs were turned round and his letters were separated and disappeared. Although by then I didn't need them any more. That we should serve in newness of spirit, and not in the oldness of the letter.

So that's how things were; but the almanac still gave us pleasure.

"King Charles XV ascended the throne on 8th July 1859." "Of the four eclipses, namely two of the sun and two of the moon, which are due to occur this year, only the second eclipse of the moon will be visible in these regions." "The market at Lycksele will be held on 10th January" and "Unless letters between all inland post-offices be franked with postage stamps to the value of twelve öre at single letter rate they cannot be accepted for dispatch."

Otherwise, they were years of scarcity then, interminable winters and frost in August and snow at midsummer and ice on Longwater on 17th June, St Botolph's Day. To whom shall we go?

"The fertility of arable land depends on its composition and suitability for the plants cultivated thereon," you, Lord, wrote in the almanac. "Only when all the conditions are fulfilled for the abundant reproduction of the plants cultivated may rich and profitable harvests be obtained from our arable fields."

Mother stripped off sallow-leaves and we picked horse-tail and sedge from the mere on Rough Marsh and she poured boiling water on it and made bran for Angel, and we had credit with Karl Orsa as well. And whenever things were at their worst, for us in our way and for Karl Orsa in his way, he would come to find mother and when he left our debts were wiped out. Owe no man any thing, but to love one another: for he that loveth another hath fulfilled the law.

"From small and insignificant seeds all living things evolve and increase and ultimately multiply and surpass the mother seed," as you wrote so beautifully in the almanac, Lord. "That is the very miracle of life itself, the miracle of fertilisation and growth and birth, which enables human beings to draw their sustenance from the soil. From a turnip seed no larger than a small grain of sand we obtain, within a few months of sowing it, a turnip weighing several pounds, not including its profuse and luxuriant haulms."

In April of '64, on Elias' day, mother bore Karl Orsa a daughter, she was given the name Tilda, in the parish register Karl Orsa was given the name Father Unknown. That spring I worked on paring down tar stumps for Nikanor in Böle, he was going to make three tar stills that summer. I got food and a

33

labourer's wages but I still didn't earn enough for the rent. I was fifteen. So that's how things were.

When Tilda was born Karl Orsa brought a china plate for her. The edge of the plate was marked in gold letters LOUISA JOSEPHINA EUGENIA.

"She's going to be called Tilda," mother said. "Not Louisa or anything else."

"It's a royal person," said Karl Orsa. "Louisa Josephina Eugenia. A princess of some kind."

He'd grown side-whiskers now and wasn't completely upright any longer but had begun to stoop a little as if he was always watching his step in a particular way, you could almost see that he was a shopkeeper and that he was constantly working something out, for he who observeth the wind shall not sow; and he that regardeth the clouds shall not reap.

"What's the idea of this plate?" asked mother. "Is it meant to be some kind of receipt?"

But that seemed to startle him and he dodged the question.

"I just thought you might like it," he said. "It's made in Germany. Genuine bone china."

"So it's not because you're her father?"

"Who the father of your children is the Lord alone knows," he said, and he almost sounded dejected as if he thought that really was the case.

"But you're the only one who's come along with a china plate," mother remarked.

"It's only by way of a memento," said Karl Orsa. "I do own your place, Thea, and we are acquainted, after all."

And mother didn't want to argue any more, that's how things were and she let it all run off her and she brought out the smoked meat and beer and said to Eva: "Come and play a couple of tunes, Eva."

And Eva played "Karl Orsa's Polka" and "The Big Boot

34

Waltz" and "The Floral Season Cometh" and "The Song of Kukumaffen", and whatever she played it sounded like a song of praise.

She was the daughter of Ol Karlsa who was Karl Orsa's father, so she was half-sister to both Tilda and her father and also an aunt to her own sister and almost like a sister-in-law to her own mother. That's how things were.

[VI]

To live without being guilty of debts is impossible, that's how you've made life, Lord. And the more we go at it and exert ourselves the larger the debt becomes, and what there is still to pay when we've done our utmost has to be left to your mercy and grace, but grace is a conditional and uncertain thing. Eva insisted on having a fiddle.

"I've got fiddle-playing hands," she said. "You can see, I was made for playing the fiddle."

And there was some truth in that: her long slender fingers seemed made for milking cows and playing the fiddle, they were darned strong and yet supple, she could bend them any way she wanted.

And Karl Orsa must have leered at her hands. Or else she'd held them out in front of him and said: "Have you seen my playing fingers? My fiddle hands?"

He bought the fiddle in Skellefteå and hung it up in his shop so that everyone who thought they had fiddle hands would see it. It was streaky brown and shiny and the bow was there too and a little green box with the resin in it, and the fiddle hung in front of the harnesses and chains and fox traps and yokes and everything else that Karl Orsa had in the shop.

"Aren't you going to give the fiddle to Eva?" he said to mother. "You've got the credit. Then you can play together. When she

36

sees the fiddle she goes as stiff as an icicle and her eyes shine and she doesn't hear you speaking to her and she can stand there for hours. Don't be unreasonable, Thea."

"If only it had been something else," mother said. "Anything .else."

She meant: If only it hadn't been music. You can deny yourself anything, but not music.

So it was more or less forced on her.

Karl Orsa came over with the fiddle himself, he'd got hold of an oblong box for it and the bow was in the box too and there was a shiny string round the box, and Eva took the fiddle and she knew what to do straight away. She'd already started to develop little titties, she put the fiddle between them and held it straight out in front of her and began tightening and plucking and tuning it – you really wouldn't have known it was the first fiddle she'd held – and then she took the bow and drew it carefully back and forth a few times across the strings, and then, believe it or not, she was playing.

And she really did have fiddle hands. Lord, how she played!

I don't remember what pieces she ran through, I don't even remember what it sounded like, I've never had a gift for music – but we were speechless and flabbergasted, mother and I and Karl Orsa. She didn't need to learn the fiddle, she knew it all from birth – you, Lord, had even made the space between her breasts just fit the body of the fiddle.

But I do remember that she played "The Song of the Lark". "Wild lark song will not last long when rain and storm o'erwhelm it."

And I remember that she bent over it so that her long shining hair touched the bow and her bowing hand, and mother went behind her and lifted her hair up so that it wouldn't get in the way of the music and plaited it and tied it in a big knot on the top of her head, and it was as if Eva was completely alone with

37

the fiddle, she didn't even notice when mother put her hair up. Karl Orsa sat on the wood-bin and leered at her – when he visited us he almost always sat on the wood-bin – the fiddle wasn't paid for yet so it was as if he owned the music, he waggled his feet and looked at her, she was thirteen and mother was over thirty, and the farmers round here have always been partial to music.

I would never have been able to hold the fiddle like Eva did, my chest is rounded and my breastbone sticks out like a chicken, due to rickets the doctor says. She never changed in that respect, as long as she lived and was able to play she held the fiddle like that, between her breasts.

What it cost I don't know: if it ever had a price in sovereigns, it was never mentioned. For mother the fiddle was more important than the price. Karl Orsa must have had some idea of what he wanted for it and it wasn't money, and you could hear straight away that it was a valuable fiddle.

During the winter that Eva got the fiddle – I was sixteen then – I was at home with a pain in my chest, there was something there that I couldn't cough up. It came in the autumn and I got weak and miserable, I couldn't manage anything more than chopping some wood and shovelling a bit of snow and mending a few pairs of shoes. If mother hadn't had her harmonium and credit and zest for life I don't know how it would have turned out. But we got through a day at a time and that's how things were and to whom shall we go, Lord? And in the evenings when it was dark mother and Eva played; and I lay with my little sisters on the ancient bed and they played right through the hymn book and dance music and the tunes they'd made up between them, I chewed resin for my chest and sucked cough drops, but the music seemed to soothe me more.

"We never need to light candles in the evenings," mother would say, "because we have the music."

She was still so full of light within herself.

In '65 and '66 she bore two children to Karl Orsa, Father Unknown. A girl first, and she gave her away to a childless couple at Brännberg, and then a stillborn boy. He was premature and apparently had brown hair like Karl Orsa. She had him when she was playing at Kusträsk. In the middle of the night, after she'd finished playing, she suddenly felt ill when they were about to carry the harmonium out, and she gave birth to him on the floor of the hall where they'd been dancing. If he'd lived she would have called him Linus after the man who used to play the psalms for the apostle Paul in the Second Epistle to Timothy.

That was the last child she had.

Later in the autumn, that autumn, Jacob came back.

Our Lord had told him to return to us, that's what he claimed. Was that really true?

He wasn't the same man any more, not the same person at all. His beard was uncut and his clothes in tatters and he didn't even have a pair of skis to travel on and it was as if he'd come because he thought he had to. He was silent and downcast, he hardly showed any interest in Sarah and Rachel even though they were his. That first evening mother was so glad to see him that she didn't realise he'd been through something that had changed him both outwardly and inwardly. She and Eva played for him and mother talked to him without noticing that he wasn't answering, and in the evening she moved the beds and made them up again so that everything should be as it was before they came to fetch him.

The rent, she seemed to be thinking, and the credit and the repayments for the fiddle, now all those trials are over. And when these things begin to come to pass, then look up, and lift up your heads; for your redemption draweth nigh. And while she was tidying up and getting things ready for the night and

39

clipping Jacob's beard she was singing softly and babbling to herself like a little girl.

And in a way all of us thought of Jacob as some kind of redeemer. The first morning after he came back I went off to see Karl Orsa. He was sitting in the parlour behind the shop and he didn't look up when I came in but I'm sure he saw me anyway.

"Jacob has come back," I said.

But Karl Orsa didn't say anything, he opened a book that was lying in front of him and leafed through it as if he was looking for a particular passage that he hadn't read.

"You remember Jacob?" I said. "The one you got them to take away?"

But it was as if he couldn't be bothered to wonder who this Jacob might be. And I felt myself becoming more and more arrogant and cocky.

"So from now on it will be nothing but cash," I said. "Remember that, Karl Orsa, nothing but money. And I'm going out to work too. So from now on."

Then he looked up and said: "So he's some kind of miracle-worker, this Jacob."

And just as I was about to answer, when he had at last started to speak, the coughing began. It was the worst coughing fit in my whole life, it came from deep inside my chest and it tore at the back of my breastbone like a hand with piercingly sharp nails. How long it lasted I don't know but I thought I was going to faint, it was as if my whole body was filled up with that cough. And at last I felt something give way inside my chest, something that came up through my throat and was the size of an egg so that my gullet was barely wide enough and when it was in my mouth the cough suddenly stopped and I spat it out in my hand. It was a black lump, absolutely round and hard. When I scratched it with a fingernail it only made a little mark on the surface.

40

And from that moment on, after that coughing fit, I recovered completely and have never felt anything in my chest since.

Karl Orsa stood up and came over and looked at the lump in my hand. "Is it blood?" he said.

"I shouldn't think so," I said. "I've never coughed up any blood before."

"But it does look rather suspect," he said. "Clotted blood."

And then it was as if he wanted to remind me of my business: "You shouldn't be going out to work yet awhile, boy. You shouldn't strain yourself. When you're coughing blood you ought to take it easy."

But I couldn't take my eyes off that black lump, everything stood still for me, I'd almost forgotten why I was there, it was as if I'd coughed away everything I'd planned, I couldn't do anything more, and in the end I went away without having settled matters with Karl Orsa. And perhaps that was just as well. I took the black lump home and mother and Jacob couldn't work out what it was either.

Mother began to notice things and soon realised that Jacob wasn't himself any longer: there was no real sense in what he said, he talked a lot about what he was going to do but nothing came of it, he was going to this or that place to work but he never set off, and he took out his tools and things and other bits and pieces and intended to mend all sorts of things that were broken, but he just left them lying around, and for long hours he would sit absent-mindedly and didn't hear her talking to him, it was as if he'd lost all his strength, and he never said a word about where they'd taken him that time when they fetched him and where he'd been all those years.

And he just couldn't do without the gin now. Karl Orsa supplied it for him. "I'll just saunter over to the shop," he would say casually, "my legs ache when I sit still like this. Is there anything you need, Thea?"

But she never did need anything, she had enough and to spare, and she knew perfectly well that a grown man couldn't just sit still doing nothing. "You go for a stroll, Jacob, I'm going to cook so there'll be a few cold potatoes for you."

When mother was thirty-five he gave her a shiny metal chain to wear round her neck.

And the gin made him so lively and good-humoured that he asked Eva to play and he took mother and danced with her; neither of them was a great dancer because mother had always been providing the music and he didn't really have the talent for it, so their dancing was rather odd and clumsy and at the end they always fell over. And he talked to me in a way he didn't usually do, of all the things we were going to tackle by and by, a horse and another cow and the ditching and adding a few tiers of logs to make a bedroom in the loft and that it might be possible to buy our home back or that there were other places we could take over or that we could abandon this place, this damned marsh, and go off to Baggböle or Holmsund and work for a company and live on the money and not have any worries, for a company worker is like a lily of the field, and that for two real men by and by nothing would be impossible. It was as if you, Lord, gave us particular special grace and strength as we sat there in the evenings; mother used to go to bed because she wasn't very interested in planning like that.

So that's how things were.

We didn't talk about the rent. The rent was only a small matter and he had some money anyway, and there was nothing special about Karl Orsa, he needn't imagine he was set up to rule like a petty king for ever, not everyone would let the ground be taken from beneath his feet by a shopkeeper who'd never been further than Skellefteå.

It was that winter that Karl Orsa changed his name to

Markström. He wanted to have a real shopkeeper's name. But nobody took any notice of it, it was just entered in the parish register.

[VII]

Lord, do you ever plan and dream the way Jacob and I did in the evenings when he'd had a drop to drink? We know it's all uncertain and yet we believe in it. Though you probably have no need to believe – the counsel of the Lord standeth for ever, the thoughts of his heart to all generations. You have marked out all things from the beginning, every last detail, and we can talk and plan things out as much as we like, your judgements rule our every step.

Karl Orsa's steps were short and careful, he walked as if he was anxious to preserve some kind of dignity, almost like a churchwarden, he really believed his name was Markström.

We knew he would come but it was still a surprise to us. Mother and Eva had been playing at Cat Hill and had come home that morning, I sat carving a doll's head for Tilda, and Jacob was lying in bed with mother and probably had a slight hangover. Karl Orsa was holding the almanac for '67 in his hand, and I thought: Jacob will get up now and bring out the money.

"So you haven't started the day yet," said Karl Orsa.

"We didn't know we were going to have an important visitor," said mother.

Then Karl Orsa said: "Love not sleep, lest thou come to poverty; open thine eyes, and thou shalt be satisfied with bread." He was well-versed in the Bible.

44

"We haven't slept," said mother. "We've been playing over at Cat Hill."

And he sat down on the wood-bin while they got up and pulled on their clothes, he seemed to have plenty of time, he leaned against the wall near the stove and flipped back and forth through his almanac, the royal family and the movements of the heavenly bodies and the commonest animal ailments; the fiddle lay there on the table, Eva had wrapped it in a cloth and it seemed to me that it looked like a baby as it lay there; it still hadn't been paid for.

Jacob sat down on the stool by the door so that he almost looked like a visitor too and mother opened the cellar hatch and took out a bottle of beer, Eva picked up the fiddle and put it away behind the bed and I put a few billets on the stove. The little girls just sat and stared at Karl Orsa as they always did when we had visitors.

And I couldn't imagine where Jacob kept the money. Perhaps he kept it in the outhouse and that was the reason why he had to sit near the door. He was unpredictable of course; he sat rubbing his blind eye, he had crumpled up and looked like the spent egg-sac of a perch, but perhaps he was still one of God's miracle-workers. He didn't want the beer that mother offered him.

"In Skellefteå they think things are going to get dearer," said Karl Orsa. "A darned sight dearer. No money's going to be enough."

"If you don't have any money you don't need to worry about high prices," said mother. "That's one advantage. When things are expensive it's worst for the ones who have money."

"You need cash for business," he said. "You can't stay in business without cash."

"Would you like some more beer?" mother said.

He passed her his mug, and then he drank as if he was really thirsty.

45

"Where's Jacob?" said mother.

And then I noticed that he wasn't sitting by the door any longer.

"He went out for a walk," I said. "His legs started aching."

I didn't want to say: he went to the outhouse to fetch the money that he'd put away. Jacob must have thought he would surprise us. He wanted to come to Karl Orsa like a thief in the night and take the ground from beneath his feet with the cash.

And you could see that mother was suddenly looking preoccupied and thoughtful. Perhaps, after all . . . ?

"And how are things generally in Skellefteå?" she said in order to talk away the time it might take before Jacob came back.

"You know how things are in Skellefteå," said Karl Orsa. "A lot of business being done and very hectic. But I can't avoid it. Because of the shop."

Mother had never been as far as Skellefteå. She'd been to Norsjö for three funerals.

"Aye," she said, "that's how it is. Skellefteå. It's like Babylon."

And they talked for quite a while about Skellefteå, about people who had gone there and not come back and the tinkers who had fought with the farmers from Bure near the church there and the parson who had drowned himself in Ursvik Creek and how folk in the town tried to talk so fine that it was almost impossible to understand what they said. And mother said that if the smoked meat hadn't been eaten up she would have brought it out and he said that he really had already eaten and that smoked meat made him colicky. But no Jacob. He must have gone to the privy first, I thought. He wants us to give up hope. But then he'll come.

"But the worst thing is the money," said Karl Orsa. "It's as if it's never enough in Skellefteå."

And now mother was pretty much at a loss.

46

"Aye," she said. "The money. It doesn't go far. That's how things are."

"So this rent of yours, Thea," he said. "It hasn't been put up since the old man died."

"Aye, that's true," said mother.

"He was so kind-hearted, the old man," said Karl Orsa. "He found it hard to charge people the right amount."

No, Jacob hadn't just gone straight to the privy. He didn't have any money in the outhouse. He didn't come back. At least not while there was still time.

"So we'll say three sovereigns more," said Karl Orsa. "I don't want to be unjust."

"It's up to you," said mother. "But I haven't got any money, you know that."

And then she said: "Johnny, you go out and see if you can find Jacob. And Eva, take Sarah and Rachel and Tilda out to the byre and mix up some bran for Angel."

But Jacob had hidden himself well. I went down through the whole village and ran halfway to Broadmere and shouted "Jacob!" into the forest, but no luck, he wasn't in the privy or in the shed, and it was so cold that the hasp on the outhouse door stuck to my hand. The same thing has happened to Jacob as happened to my father, I thought, he's gone mad, if he survives this and comes back they'll have to send him away to Pitholmen, mother has darned bad luck with her men.

When I got home I saw that Karl Orsa hadn't gone yet, his dogskin coat was lying against the windowpane, so I went to the byre and helped Eva to make the bran for Angel.

After a while mother came and said that he'd gone now and that it was strange of Jacob just to disappear like that, he wasn't dressed for the cold, and now we should go in and boil potatoes

47

and Karl Orsa had had a piece of pork brawn in the pocket of his fur coat that we could have with them.

On the table lay the almanac for '67 and the pork brawn and a piece of cloth for Tilda and a sugar-loaf.

In the evening after we'd gone to bed Jacob came back. He was so cold that he could barely walk. He sat down on the stool by the door where he'd sat before he went out and he didn't say a word, but mother got up and took hold of him and led him to the bed and he lay down without taking off his clothes and in the end she managed to get some life back into him.

But in the morning when we woke he'd gone again and mother hadn't noticed him getting out of bed, but we said he's sure to come back because he can't stand the cold.

But by midday he still hadn't come. Then someone came over from the shop, one of Karl Orsa's servant girls, and said that mother had to come, it was about Jacob.

When we got there the first thing we saw was Jacob. You couldn't help seeing him. He was sitting on top of the chimney-stack of Karl Orsa's house, sitting quite still with his head in his hands looking neither up nor down. The people of the house were standing in the yard staring at him. Karl Orsa's house is huge and his chimneystack is higher than all the other chimney-stacks, it was as if Jacob had tried to retreat as high up as possible, as if he'd been trying to reach the utmost point – Lord, to whom shall we go?

"Is that a gun he's got across his knees?" mother asked.

"It's a muzzle loader," said Karl Orsa.

"He hasn't got a gun," said mother.

"He came early this morning and wanted to buy.it," said Karl Orsa. "And I gave it to him on credit. And a powder-horn and black powder and fuses and a bag of shot."

"Is he going to shoot himself?" someone asked.

"He won't," said mother.

48

And they started to say that he'd probably freeze to death, he didn't have enough clothes on and up there in the sky it was absolutely clear and cold, even colder than down on the ground where we were standing. But then Karl Orsa said that as long as they kept the stove burning there was no risk of that, Jacob was warmer than the rest of us, you could even see the wispy blue smoke behind his back from the birchwood and alderwood that they were burning. So no fear of that.

And some of us went up so close that we could only see his head above the roof, and we shouted to him to come to his senses, you heard us Lord, we told him to throw away the gun and we'd give him the ladder that he'd kicked away and he could climb down, because it was totally pointless sitting up there on the chimneystack. Karl Orsa went in and brought out some gin and held it up and said he'd get a drink if he came down, and I shouted to him that by and by, and the horse that we'd get, and the little room in the loft, and the marshy patch behind the byre, and Baggböle and Holmsund . . . and a man from Kläppen who was a cousin of Karl Orsa and married to a half-sister of Nikanor of Böle shouted that he ought to have pity on his children and come on down, for all little children need a father, he'd had mumps himself and hadn't had any children. But it was as if Jacob was deaf and blind, he didn't even shake his head, he just sat there absolutely still.

And of course folks living nearby heard that Thea's Jacob had climbed up on to Karl Orsa's chimneystack and that he was sitting there now with a gun and that anything might happen, no one knew how it would finish, for God's Creation is unending. So a lot of people came along to see Jacob, and they made a fire in the middle of the yard and stood there warming their hands and talking, and the crowd thought he'd simply gone mad and that he would presumably climb down eventually. And someone said it was probably Karl Orsa who'd hired him to do a crazy thing like that to get people to his shop. And someone knew that the same thing had happened to a man at Avaträsk, he went to sleep and fell down and was killed; people who sat on top of chimneystacks shouldn't be allowed to fall asleep.

But when they started saying that he might use the gun and that he could shoot dead anyone he wanted from up there, they got rather uneasy in the yard and several of them went inside the shop so as not to get shot. But then mother said: "He's no marksman. He's lost his aiming eye."

Some of them were invited in to eat at Karl Orsa's. They got roast meat, you could smell it when they opened the door.

And Jacob just sat where he was, you wouldn't have known that he usually got aches and pains from sitting still.

In the afternoon Karl Orsa hit on the idea of smoking him down with straw. And it really did give off horrible smoke, Jacob and the chimneystack disappeared completely, the smoke settled like a dense black cloud over the roof and we said: "Now, dammit!" But then a little gust of wind came and blew it all away and there he was again still sitting there.

As evening came it began to snow, and when it got dark we went home. Karl Orsa set two men to look after the fire and keep a sort of watch. In the morning when it was light he wasn't sitting on the chimneystack any more – how he'd managed to get down nobody knows, you couldn't see anything because of the fresh snow – and he'd stood the gun against the wall by the door.

That same day Karl Orsa came over with the gun.

"No one will want this gun," he said, "not after this. So I thought that you, Thea . . ."

"What do I want with a gun?" said mother.

"Your boy. Johnny. At least he can shoot some squirrels."

"Isn't it a bit expensive?" mother said.

"You've got credit, Thea," said Karl Orsa.

And I was pleased, of course. The snow was fresh, I tried it by shooting at a knot in the wall of the byre, I saw a hare down the hill but didn't have time to light the fuse, and I shot two squirrels just this side of Long Marsh.

[VIII]

And I must tell you about how mother and Eva were paid for their playing: sometimes they got a shoulder of mutton or a piece of pork or a leg of veal, and sometimes they got cash. One of the dancers would go round with a cap just like taking a collection in church; they mostly got small coppers but sometimes a silver coin too. At the beginning of the week one of us took the money to Karl Orsa and he counted it and wrote it down in the book where the debts were recorded.

Jacob had had a page to himself in the book, mother found that out after he'd disappeared. It was mostly gin, but also a pair of boots and a shiny metal necklace and four packets of snuff.

"I've crossed out his name and put yours instead, Thea," said Karl Orsa. "That's how it is with debts – someone has to take them over."

"You can have the necklace back again," said mother. "And cross it out in the book."

"Necklaces don't sell," replied Karl Orsa. "Jacob was the only one. Nobody else wants them. That's the sort of man Jacob was."

And about the credit he said: "Don't think you're the only one, Thea. Hardly anyone's free of debt. I even have big farmers in the book. A faithful man shall abound with blessings: but he that maketh haste to be rich shall not be innocent, so hardly anyone's free of debt."

"But you, Karl Orsa, don't have any debts," mother remarked.

"Money debts," said Karl Orsa, "but they're a special kind."

And he went on: "Not to mention interest. Even Jesus Christ said you should charge interest. That you were bad and lazy if you didn't make sure you received interest. If you owe a debt to the Lord then you have to make sure you receive his forgiveness now and then, and the interest on a money debt is like God's forgiveness for the fact that you can't repay it all at once."

"And when do you want the interest?" mother said.

"For you I don't count the interest. I couldn't do that."

In the summer of '67 the potatoes froze in July and the spring had come so late that the barley didn't set ears till August and by then it was already frostbitten. In September we slaughtered the ewe, there was already snow then and by October the ice on the lake was thick enough to walk on. We wouldn't have survived that winter without your mercy, Lord, and Karl Orsa's credit, it was as if you and Karl Orsa had agreed to keep us alive; he said he came for the music and inside his dogskin coat he carried potatoes and pieces of pork and flour and even sugar – he usually came once a week and made sure no one knew what he had in his coat, and each time he came we had to go out for a while and mother paid off some of the debt. So while folk were starving everywhere else we managed reasonably well; I shot a hare now and then and we had dried fish and there was firewood so we didn't freeze. Mother had only three engagements during the whole of that winter and those were funerals, they didn't want the fiddle, just the harmonium, they didn't think you could play funeral music on the fiddle, but she wasn't paid anything, you don't pay for funeral music.

But they were good times for Karl Orsa. In the spring he took over the whole of Böle village and half of Kläppen, five thousand acres of forest and ploughland and marshes and hay-meadows, and how it happened I'm not quite sure, only that when the winter was over it was his. And by June he was the only man who had enough seed-corn both for himself and to sell.

One day in the autumn of '67 as we sat eating mother felt something sharp in her mouth and when she took it out it was a tooth, and she laughed and said it was really high time she lost her milk-teeth. But after that a tooth fell out almost every day, and before Christmas she hadn't a single one left; the day she was thirty-six she lost her last tooth. And it was as if her face shrivelled up and she became an old woman.

"Have you lost your teeth?" said Karl Orsa. "And you who were such a beauty."

How large the debt was when that winter was over I don't know, it must have been frightful, it can't still have been on a single page in Karl Orsa's book, perhaps he'd now opened a separate book just for us.

He came about the rent in the New Year, and from that day on I didn't understand you at all, Lord. It was so cold that the pedals had frozen on the harmonium so it couldn't be played and we sat round the stove to keep ourselves warm. But when Karl Orsa came Eva brought out the fiddle straight away, as there was nothing wrong with that, and she put it between her tits and played, and we didn't talk because Karl Orsa wanted it to be that way; like King Saul he was refreshed by the music and was well. He sat with his hands stretched towards the stove and waggled his boots and leered at Eva.

When she stopped to rest her fingers for a moment he turned round to mother and said: "How old would she be now? Seventeen?"

"She's fifteen," mother said. "But big for her age."

"You've suddenly aged, Thea," he said.

And mother had to agree: "Time passes no one by and no one gets any younger."

54

And she added: "But you're in good shape, Karl Orsa."

And it was true, he was in good shape, he had filled out a bit and looked well-fed, his hair was still black and glossy and his face was smooth apart from the furrows on the brow that he'd always had.

"Perhaps we ought to settle up," he said. "Our business."

"Shouldn't I get the beer?" mother said. "And Eva has made up some new tunes that you haven't heard."

"I've thought a lot about you, Thea," he said. "You ought to give some things up. Your boy will soon be twenty. And your oldest girl's grown up. So that you don't have so many worries."

"I've got nothing to give up," mother said. "What should I give up?"

"You've got the debts, Thea. And the rent."

"That's how things are," mother said. "And we do our best. None of us can do any more."

And then he said quite plainly what he was thinking: "I want to settle things with Eva from now on. If Johnny can't get the money together. But it would be easiest to settle with Eva. And I'm not a wicked man."

When mother realised what he meant she went as pale as death and stood up from her chair and was a little unsteady on her feet as if she was going to faint, and then she walked across the floor and lay down on the bed and nobody said a word.

Lord, to whom shall we go?

But then at last she sat up on the bed and said: "Never. I'd rather you killed me, Karl Orsa."

"What pleasure would I get from killing you, Thea?" he said. "I don't want anything bad, I just want to settle things."

"My children aren't shop-goods," she said. "My children aren't horseshoe-nails and cotton cloth and twists of tobacco. And they're not money."

55

He was silent for a while. But then he said, and he sounded both pitiful and eager to get what he wanted: "But I've taken a fancy to her. Do you understand that, Thea, I've taken a fancy to her."

And then mother said – and she thought that would be the end of the matter: "She's your half-sister. Ol Karlsa was her father. You're her half-brother. The nakedness of thy sister, the daughter of thy father, or daughter of thy mother, thou shalt not uncover. For whosoever shall commit this abomination their souls shall be cut off from among their people."

But he wasn't a shopkeeper for nothing, he had thought the matter over and prepared himself: "I've spoken to the parson," he said. "She has no father. 'Father unknown', said the parson. So it can't be Ol Karlsa, he wasn't unknown."

And mother fell silent. That's how things were. Answer not a fool according to his folly, lest thou also be like unto him. Karl Orsa was possessed, she wasn't going to argue with him.

"But if you don't want an arrangement, Thea," he said, "then debt-recovery proceedings are all that's left. Justice has to take its course. Then there's nothing I can do."

"There's nothing here to take," mother said.

"A sheep," said Karl Orsa. "And a cow for slaughter. And the harmonium. And the fiddle."

"You can take all of them," said mother. "But you don't touch Eva."

Then he stood up and got ready to go, and when he had put on his fur coat he went up to Eva and took the fiddle out of her hands and put it under his arm, and as he stood in the doorway he said: "Think it over again, Thea. For your own sake and for the children's."

When he'd gone there was utter silence, none of us knew what to do or what to say. Finally mother said: "The Lord can surely still perform miracles. And if you abandon hope you abandon everything."

And she took the sheep's tallow that I kept for the gun and greaséd the pedal mechanism in the harmonium so the pedals would move and then she started to play, and she didn't play hymns but dance music and happy tunes, and she even sang "The Song of Kukumaffen" for us, and it seemed a little easier to breathe and as if Karl Orsa didn't really have the power to do whatever he wanted with us. I've never been able to produce a single tune all my life, not so much as a verse of a hymn, you know that, Lord, but even so I wouldn't have been alive today if it hadn't been for music.

And Sarah and Rachel brought out the pine cones and made pigs and cows and goats on the floor for Tilda.

But when mother had gone to the byre Eva put on her coat and went out, and I thought she was just going for a short walk so she didn't have to sit thinking about the fiddle and everything else. But when mother came back from the byre she still hadn't returned.

And mother had got things ready for the night and tucked Tilda in by the time she came, and when she did at last come she was carrying the fiddle under her arm and had the almanac for '68 in her hand.

Mother didn't say anything, she just went to the bed and lay down on her stomach and her whole body shook as if she was freezing to death, and when at last she sat up she was as old in the face as grandmother was just before she died.

To whom shall we go?

But Eva sat down by the stove and went over the fiddle with her fingers as if to check that it wasn't damaged, and she turned the pegs and tuned it more carefully and exactly than she'd ever done before. Then she began to play, and it actually was possible to play funeral music on the fiddle after all: "Cankered by

57

the worm unseen, Blooms will soon from cheeks be taken,
And the fruit, though it be green, From the bough by wind is
shaken."

[IX]

Lord, I've racked my brains a lot about Karl Orsa's book-keeping.
How did he set about deciding that one of our debts had been
paid, how did he work it out? Everything has its price, and
someone has to set the price, since the price isn't part of the
world order, and how Karl Orsa went about it I don't know,
perhaps it was simply that his body was like a steelyard and a
measuring-rod. They say that in the beginning of time the human
body was the only thing that could be used when something had
to be measured. "And with what measure ye mete, it shall be
measured to you," are your own words, Lord, and that saying
must have applied to Karl Orsa too.

Eva was very like mother, they had the same fair glossy hair
and they were both light of body and light of heart, you'd have
said nothing was impossible for them, they were both nimble
and they never had to think for long when something needed
doing, it was as if their body and soul was one and the same
thing.

For me it's always been as if my body has never quite kept up
with my soul.

If mother and Eva had been the same age they could have
been sisters. But mother soon got old, in both body and mind.
When Karl Orsa decided he wanted Eva because she was somehow worth more than mother it was a blow to mother and she
never got over it, never got over the fact that she wasn't good

59

enough and that she couldn't protect Eva any longer. A month must have gone by without her touching the harmonium and she didn't seem to enjoy listening to Eva playing.

"And she's nothing but a child," she said.

Apart from that she didn't say anything, she was so quiet that it was a bit worrying, and she withdrew into herself so that it sometimes almost felt as if she was a stranger.

On Good Friday Karl Orsa arrived, and it was obvious that he'd come on some special kind of errand. He sat down on the wood-bin and said nothing, but his eyes went over us as if he wanted to see whether we could bear to hear the reason for his visit, and he almost seemed a bit excited; mother said nothing either and she never brought out the beer these days.

And finally, when he realised that we really were beginning to wonder why he'd come, he said it: "Well – old Jacob. They've found him."

And there he paused for a moment, he wanted to make the most of his news and not get it over with all at once. Mother was standing by the table and it looked as if she wasn't paying any attention, but she was standing stock still.

"They found him at Baggböle. Down by the river, in a pine tree."

And then he fell silent again, just as if he had to search his memory to recall what he knew.

"He'd hanged himself," he said at last. "With a bridle."

And then there was total silence, we didn't know what to do, that's how things were. Sarah and Rachel crept up on the bed and sat with their arms round one another, they did that sometimes, and I thought about Karl Orsa and tried to understand what he really wanted.

In the end mother said, about Jacob: "And he who was so afraid of everything."

60

That was all that was said, and what she really meant I don't know.

And then Karl Orsa left, he had no other business with us that time, it was as if we'd somehow paid off a little bit of our debt just by being there to listen to what he had to say. He didn't say that he wanted Eva to go with him to the shop about the debts, that was what he used to do these days, he had always settled the accounts with mother at our place, but he wanted Eva to come to the little parlour behind the shop.

There be three things which are too wonderful for me, yea, four which I know not: the way of an eagle in the air, the way of a serpent upon a rock, the way of a ship in the midst of the sea, and the way of a man with a maid.

In the summer of '68 Angel swelled up with bloat the first time she ate clover and we had to slaughter her. But we got a heifer on credit from Karl Orsa, she was called Taphath after a daughter of King Solomon, she was small and only had three teats but still turned out to be a good milker, though it was difficult to milk her because your fingers were always groping for the teat that wasn't there.

And that same summer the farmers at Risträsk and Heda built a frame-saw by Stony Brook, it had two blades and an edger for trimming; they'd got relief payments for the year of famine and had some money left over and used it to build the saw. In the autumn Karl Orsa came and told mother that there was something for Johnny to do now, really good earnings, and that he would talk to the Risträsk farmers, there was work for all sorts of people at a sawmill, he even knew of women who worked in the sawmills. And I said I was fit enough for work, if there was a job going, and it didn't have to be women's work, I was a grown man and a frame-saw was nothing special.

And so I got a job as an assistant to the stackers, I stood on top of the stacks and laid out the sawn timber, and I got three crowns a week. But by October the sawing was finished and then it was felling in the forest; during the winter they had to cut the timber that was needed for sawing the next summer, and you earned less money in the forest.

And that was the last winter that mother went out playing the harmonium. She'd begun to get some trouble in her fingers, and you know how it was, Lord, they went stiff and wouldn't serve her properly as they used to, she often sat holding them up in front of her and looking at them, but nothing showed on the outside.

"They won't obey me any more," she said. "It's as if you can't talk to them."

She could still manage hymn tunes and dance music if it wasn't too fast, but a schottische or a fast polka was impossible; the dancers could hear things go wrong sometimes, and nothing is more important than the rhythm. So when they came over from Arnberg just before Christmas wanting music for a Saturday night they said they could get by with Eva and the fiddle, there weren't that many of them and it would be much simpler in a way and it couldn't be much fun for her, since she wasn't so young any more, to have to be running backwards and forwards like a shuttle playing dance music.

"There's nothing I like better than playing the harmonium," mother said.

"But still," said the dancers from Arnberg.

And then mother realised that that's how things were, her music wasn't even worth a few coins any more, it wasn't worth the trouble of putting the harmonium on a sledge behind a horse, so she said no more and Eva went to play at Arnberg on her own.

She wanted me to go along when Eva went off to play. So if I was at home I did, it was something to do, anyway, although I wasn't a dancer, and anyone who tried to teach me soon gave up, and then I would sit beside Eva and listen to the music and fetch water for her when she was thirsty, and support her back when she got tired, and if I closed my eyes I hardly noticed them dancing and having a good time.

And mother went on playing for herself, preferably when she was alone at home so that no one could hear her. "My fingers may recover again," she said. "Our Lord can do anything he wants, perhaps he intends my fingers not to move so quickly, religious music never goes quickly."

In April '69 I took the money that I'd earned that winter and went to Karl Orsa and laid it on his table in the little parlour behind the shop.

He looked at it thoughtfully for a moment, and then said: "What's this money for?"

"It's to pay off some of the debt," I said.

And then he thought for a while again. "You should be careful with money," he said. "You shouldn't just chuck money away like that."

"I want you to write it down in the book," I said. "And deduct it from our debt."

He was always slow to speak, and now he was even slower than usual. "No," he said. "It's not worth opening a book for that amount of money."

"It's as much as a year's rent," I said.

"Eva's already paid the rent," he said. "And don't worry yourself about the credit."

"You just take the money," I said. "And write it down in the book."

"I won't take it," he said. "And what I write in the book is no concern of yours."

And then I thought: I'm not arguing with him any more, I'll never get to understand him, he moves like a serpent upon a rock, that's how he is, so I left the money lying on the table, said

63

no more and went off, and he couldn't think of anything more to say either.

Some days later I was chopping up winter firewood on the slope above the farm fence, and when I came in one evening mother said that Karl Orsa had called by and given Tilda a fistful of coins, and I saw the money and recognised it straight away, and I told mother that she shouldn't have accepted it. But he'd been so obstinate, she hadn't been able to give it back, he was pig-headed as well as everything else, and why he'd done it was a mystery to her.

"To think that you can even get money on credit," mother said.

[X]

Mother was always so worried about Eva, it was as if she thought Eva had some kind of weakness although she was so quick and hard-working and never ever complained about anything. Maybe it was because Eva was her eldest daughter and because she had all that music in her soul and in her hands, it was as if mother thought Eva was more sensitive than an ordinary person. So she kept asking her whether she could feel pain anywhere and whether she was cold and whether she'd eaten enough and whether she'd slept as she should during the night, and after her own fingers had begun to stiffen she asked Eva several times a day whether she could feel anything strange in her fingers, and it sounded as if she expected what had happened to her to happen to Eva as well. And even when she didn't say anything you could see her turning things over in her mind, her eyes were worried and enquiring when she looked at Eva. After things had turned out as they had with Karl Orsa she always wanted to know about Eva's periods, whether they came when they should and whether they seemed the same as usual, and Eva probably never understood why mother worried the way she did, she didn't have it in her to be afraid of anything evil, innocence shall guide the meek and whoever leads a blameless life shall live securely.

In the summer of '69 I was only at home for the haymaking and we moved no more than thirty hay-racks in all. The rest of the time I was at the sawmill at Stony Brook, I was now earning four crowns a week and was called a stacker, though mostly I stood on top of the stacks taking the sawn timber from the stackers who were bigger than me. I took my wages home to mother and what she did with the money I don't know, Karl Orsa wouldn't accept our money these days, so what use was it to us? He'd pushed us so far that he'd abolished money for us. Lord, what was your purpose in creating credit?

Mother was now thirty-eight, Eva was seventeen, Sarah fourteen and Rachel twelve and I was twenty. Tilda was five. In August Karl Orsa found jobs for Sarah and Rachel in service, they needed to get away from home and do their bit, he said. Rachel was a little sad because she'd just started learning to play the harmonium. Sarah went to Aggträsk and Rachel to Björknäset.

That autumn Karl Orsa was ill for a while and got it into his head that he was going to die. It was inside his belly, a kind of lump behind his navel, he thought it was cancer and he even pulled up his shirt once to show us where it was, but there was nothing to see. While he went around dying like that he often came over to our place, for no particular reason – unless you'd call the cancer and music reasons of a sort. He would sit there in silence on the wood-bin and would want mother to play for him even though it sounded the way it did. Eva was left in peace at that time except that he wanted her to play the fiddle for him, "Now my hours of life declining Move towards their peaceful goal."

And mother told him he ought to get some tansy that was in flower then and dry the blossoms and eat them, and put them in his gin too, so that if he made sure he drank a lot and peed a lot it would probably do some good – she knew they'd done that in the old days and that it was like a miracle cure – and he could keep the blossoms in a bag and let them lie on his belly at night when he slept.

"I can't sleep at nights," was his response to that, and he sounded miserable.

"That may well be for reasons other than your belly," said mother.

To which he replied: "It'll be my cousin's children at Gallejaur who'll inherit it all from me. And they don't understand a thing about business."

And: "I'll tear your debt out of the book, Thea. When I'm gone you'll be as free of debt as a newborn babe."

And he seemed even better versed in the Bible than usual: "Take no thought for your life," he said, "what ye shall eat, nor yet for your body, what ye shall put on. Life is more than meat, and the body more than raiment."

Mother should never have told him about tansy. It must have been the dried blossoms that made him well. I can't believe that you, Lord, performed a miracle with Karl Orsa.

Though who can fathom him who is wise and mighty and removeth mountains and they know not and shaketh the earth out of her place, and the pillars thereof tremble?

He stayed away for a while and then he came and said he wanted Eva to go with him to the shop again, there was still a lot to be sorted out and settled, and what had happened to the lump behind his navel we never found out, and mother said that of all people on earth whoremongers live the longest.

They got a new servant-girl at Karl Orsa's that autumn, she was called Johanna, and I went over there to have a look at her when she first arrived. She was small and thin with yellowish brown hair, but she had big tits and her eyes were quick and sort of restless, she came from Åmsele.

And she was easy to talk to, we soon got acquainted, she called me Johan and nobody else has ever done that. When she heard that we'd got a harmonium and a fiddle she said she'd come and see us when she had time, for music was the only thing that made her really feel like a human being, she had an uncle at Mårdsele who had a harmonium and she'd played on it when she was little.

What is man, that thou shouldest magnify him and that thou shouldest set thine heart upon him? And that thou shouldest visit him every morning, and try him every moment? That Johanna was like a revelation to me, if they hadn't come and sent her down to the cellar to fetch turnips I could have stayed there all day talking to her. And then she came over on Sundays, when she was given some time off in the afternoon, and she and Eva soon became friends. She could play too, and mother taught her everything she didn't already know and after only a month it sounded as if she'd never done anything else than play the harmonium. So when they came from Brinkliden and wanted Eva to come and play, Eva said she wanted to take Johanna and the harmonium with her, and the farmers' lads from Brinkliden said that would be all right as long as there was no extra charge, the farmers in this area have always been partial to music. And that's how it was from then on, they played together, and Karl Orsa said he didn't interfere in what his servant-girls got up to as long as they didn't lead an immoral life.

And mother scrutinised Eva regularly night and morning to see if anything had happened to her, and I know for a fact that she constantly spoke to you, Lord, about her not getting in the family way, for she was sure neither you nor she could stand that, and she tried to talk to Karl Orsa but he showed no compassion. "When it's a matter of business," he said, "you can't be lenient or sensitive." But Eva seemed to tell herself that that's how things were and that if thine enemy be hungry, give him bread to eat; and if he be thirsty, give him water to drink; for thou shalt heap coals of fire upon his head. It was as if she'd been born just for that: to play the fiddle and to take care of our debts.

68

And eventually mother almost began to believe Eva was barren. Actually we never talked about what was unavoidable – why talk and argue about things you can't prevent?

[XI]

I'll tell you all of it just as it was.

After New Year in 1870 I went to Baggböle and got a job there as a stacker, though Lindström, who was in charge of the timber-yard, thought I was on the small side. On 9th March, Forty Martyrs' Day, I fell down from a stack, I fell headfirst and the pad I was wearing on my left shoulder took the brunt of it, but I broke a bone in my chest so I couldn't move my arm. I got a lift from a carter from Lycksele, and got off the wagon at Åmsele and found out where Johanna's house was. Her father was working at Betsele, but her mother was at home – she was incredibly fat – sitting by the stove cutting up dried fish for the dogs.

"Johanna comes to our place a lot," I said. "She plays the harmonium."

"She's always been mad on music," she said. "But we hope she'll turn out decent and respectable."

"The harmonium is mostly used for playing hymns," I said.

"We all know what it's like with music," she said. "Maybe it's all right for them that sing a hymn now and again. But them that play . . ."

"My mother's played all her life," I said.

"I don't know her," said Johanna's mother. "So I couldn't say."

"A lot of folk find a kind of happiness in music," I said. "Mother's always comforted herself with music."

"But how've things turned out for her?" said Johanna's mother. "How's she got on in life?"

I said no more after that, we could have argued endlessly about music, the dogs were fighting over the dried fish, she didn't ask about Johanna and she didn't even ask who I was or where I came from, nor did she notice that my left arm was hanging straight down like the weight in a clock, and I was hungry but she didn't bring out so much as a crust of bread. So after a while I left without us having become better acquainted, the dogs followed me to the door and barked – they were elkhounds, Johanna's father used to hunt elk. I stopped over with a farming couple at Ajaur for the night and they gave me some barley porridge.

The bone in my chest didn't mend again until that summer, I went around the whole spring without being able to do a thing, at first I couldn't even hunt, and mostly I sat talking to mother or went across to the shop now and then – Johanna had to help out there a lot because Karl Orsa was always buying in more and more of everything, so one of the servant-girls had to be in the shop all the time.

"You're here in the shop a lot," Karl Orsa said to me once. "You shouldn't strain your credit."

"I'm not buying anything," I said. "I'm just looking around."

"That can be costly too," he said. "Looking around."

"Do you want to drive your customers away?" I said.

"You shouldn't be so touchy," he answered, because he saw I was riled. "You've got to learn to take a bit of teasing, Johnny."

And then he took out half a sugar-loaf and told me to take it home for Tilda. Lord, thou who searchest all hearts and understandeth all the imaginations of the thoughts, did you ever understand Karl Orsa?

While I was going around being useless with that arm of mine, in the spring of '70, Johanna told me one Sunday evening that

71

they'd moved her to the little room behind the kitchen and that she was alone there at night. So I went and stood outside in the yard behind the big mountain ash waiting till I saw they'd blown out the last candle at Karl Orsa's – and I didn't have to wait long because they always went to bed early to save the tallow and candle-grease – and then I went in to Johanna. She'd already undressed and gone to bed. I remember she laughed at me when I said that the worst thing was that arm of mine that made me less of a man than I would have been normally.

She was the first woman I lay with. And the only one.

Mother realised straight away how things were between me and Johanna. And she tried to tell me what I should do to make things go all right so I wouldn't get Johanna in the family way, to be as careful as when you're carving the handle on a cup, though it was pretty much too late by then anyway.

And Eva wasn't barren. Just before Easter mother was quite sure, she knew all the signs and she could never be mistaken, and then she was so heartbroken that she didn't get up for two days. But on the third day, when Eva came in from the byre after milking Taphath, mother got up and dressed and put a black shawl over her hair and went over to Karl Orsa. He said they could go into the parlour if there was something to be discussed.

"So that's how things are," mother said. "With Eva."

But he didn't seem to understand.

"She was quite fit and lively when I last saw her," he said.

"She must be in her third month," said mother. "You had her over here the last Saturday before Lent. That's when it happened."

"I only talked to her," said Karl Orsa. "We talked about your debts, Thea. And I gave her a piece of cloth for an apron."

"I can take you to court, Karl Orsa," said mother.

"Better not," he said. "With your debts. And I can take an

oath. But you can never take an oath about your debts. And who would keep you then?"

"Johnny will soon be fit," mother said. "His arm has nearly mended."

"He's got enough troubles of his own," said Karl Orsa. "And even with two arms he's hardly a Samson."

"A father must take responsibility for his children," mother said. "That's a duty before Our Lord."

"And who would believe you, Thea?" said Karl Orsa. "You who've had six bastards yourself. And Eva going out playing at dances?"

"If you were as careful with your cock as you are with everything else this would never have happened," mother said.

"I haven't got any debts," he said. "I run the shop carefully so that I'll never get into debt."

"Eva is your sister," said mother. "And it is written that thou shalt not uncover the nakedness of thy father's daughter or the nakedness of thy mother's daughter."

"I've spoken to the parson," said Karl Orsa. "I'm not related to Eva in any way."

"You shouldn't have asked the parson," said mother. "You should have asked Ol Karlsa, your father, while he was alive."

"He handed over everything to me," said Karl Orsa. "And he didn't say a word about any child."

"Eva's child will have his uncle, the brother of his own mother, for a father," said mother. "And he'll be a brother of his mother's sisters. And Eva will be his aunt as well as his mother. And he'll be his own cousin."

"It won't be a boy," said Karl Orsa. "Bastards are hardly ever boys."

"You'll be her uncle and her father," said mother. "And you know what inbreeding means. Have you thought about that?"

73

And now he really did think about it, it was as if he did finally take in a little bit of what mother had said.

"It is written," he said at last, "that if any man will sue thee at the law, and take away thy coat, let him have thy cloak also. So I'll delete what's in the book, Thea. I'll mark it down that the fiddle is fully paid for. And the heifer. Not because I owe you anything, but for the love of Our Lord."

"And nothing else?" said mother.

"That's already going a lot further than what's really a sensible deal," he said.

"How will you be able to answer for this?" said mother.

"As long as your books are in order," said Karl Orsa, "you have nothing to fear on the day of reckoning."

And then they both fell silent, it was as if it was hard to think of anything else to say. But in the end Karl Orsa said: "Your boy Johnny has got one of my servant-girls in the family way. You haven't got your children under very good control, Thea."

And mother said nothing.

"He doesn't look like a whoremonger," said Karl Orsa. "But even so."

And what could mother have said?

"I don't want my servant-girls to have bastards," he went on. "It's not good for business. People talk something terrible."

"So people's gossip is your only yardstick, is it?" said mother.

"But I've been thinking about it," he said. "They may need help. And I'm not one to bear a grudge."

"What am I to do?" was the only thing mother could think of saying. "What am I to do?"

"If you send Johnny over here I'll talk to him," said Karl Orsa. "We'll arrange for everything to be done right and proper. As it should be."

And mother had given up completely. To whom shall we go?

So she just turned and left the parlour and walked out through

74

the shop, she'd taken off her black shawl since she no longer cared if anyone saw that her hair was grey, and Karl Orsa followed her. When they got to the door she finally recovered herself and said: "You're unnatural. You're like the way of a serpent upon a rock."

"I don't want my house to be a den of vice," said Karl Orsa. "That's all."

So later that evening I went to Karl Orsa and he told me and Johanna how everything would be arranged, we'd get a ride with a load of barley flour to Norsjö and ask for the banns to be published and then we'd get married in the parsonage when the period of notice was over, and I could have his black suit which he didn't use any more and Johanna could wear the Sunday dress that she wore when she was playing at dances. He knew exactly what we had to do although he wasn't married himself and had no intention whatever of being crazy enough to get married, and we could have the rings on credit. And I was quite flabbergasted, we are troubled on every side, yet not distressed, we are perplexed, but not in despair, persecuted, but not forsaken, cast down, but not destroyed, and my bad arm was still hanging down like the weight in a clock.

[XII]

I exercised my left arm again by walking in the forest with my gun. If I had to act fast when a hare or a squirrel appeared in front of me my arm forgot it was injured and did everything almost as it should, it was the gun that healed my arm, and I shot enough small game for Karl Orsa to value their pelts at ten crowns.

Johanna had to leave Karl Orsa's and she moved in with us. Rachel's and Sarah's bed was still there and one extra mouth to feed made no difference, we had credit, and Eva and Johanna said the babes they were carrying would be like brother and sister. And they pressed each other's bellies and felt the unborn infants kicking against their hands.

Eva grew absurdly big and she ate as much as two grown men, but Johanna only got a little bit rounder, as if she was putting on some weight, that's all.

When we'd finished with the hay and I'd chopped the wood for the winter I got a job at the sawmill by Stony Brook. That lasted into October.

On 27th October Johanna's time came. Mother helped her and everything went quickly and smoothly as if she'd already had a lot of children. It was a girl and Johanna wanted her to be called Sabina because it was the name-day she was born on. Karl Orsa gave her a china plate that had "Sophia" written on it, she was the crown princess.

But things didn't go so well for Eva.

Lord, nobody's books are in such good order as yours, nothing is ever crossed out. If grace exists you keep it to yourself and well hidden, I don't understand it. It is written that God resisteth the proud, and giveth grace to the humble. Should Eva have been even more humble than she was? Perhaps it was her music that wasn't humble enough? When she was confined she wanted to have the fiddle on her belly, she couldn't use the bow of course, but she lay plucking it with her fingers so that you could still make out the tunes she was thinking. "For life's short span of pain and mirth I cannot be intended, Not just a worm to creep on earth, Its progress there soon ended." And "In a field the maiden turned hay with her rake, 'Gladly,' the swain said, 'I'd die for your sake.'"

When her pains began I took Tilda and went out to the byre. I had a piece of charcoal and wrote letters on the logs for her to learn, she was six years old and a really fast learner. When we'd written all the letters and all our names and I couldn't think what else to do, mother came and said that things weren't going as they should with Eva, nothing was happening, I was to go at once and fetch Erik's Hannah, who was the one usually called for at births.

So that's what I did, and Tilda was left alone with Taphath in the byre. Hannah said she'd had a feeling someone would be needing her, she said that to everyone who came, she just sat by the window doing nothing.

Eva was lying in bed when we got there, not moving, and she paid no attention to us, she was enormous, it was the first time I'd seen a woman in labour. Johanna was sitting on the wood-bin giving suck to Sabina, I remember it so well.

And Erik's Hannah went up to her and squeezed her belly and laid her cheek against it to see if she could hear anything, and she didn't notice me still being there. And she opened her

77

slit as if she could look right inside her body, and she squeezed and slapped the outside of her belly over and over again and laid her cheek against it. Then finally she said: "There's no life in that one. It'll be stillborn. And the size of two newborn babies."

Nothing showed in mother's face, hardly anything ever showed these days, they stood quite still and looked at Eva, both mother and Erik's Hannah. But at last mother said: "Are you sure there's no life there?"

That was the first thing she thought of: life.

"It's as dead as a stone."

And only then did mother speak of Eva: "Will she be able to give birth to it?"

"Not without help," said Erik's Hannah. "If then, even."

And she said she wanted soap or sheep's tallow for her hands so that she wouldn't hurt Eva more than necessary. I went out to the byre to Tilda, Taphath had settled down and Tilda was lying against her stomach asleep, I sat down beside her and I think I could hear Eva all the way out there. When mother came I'd fallen asleep too.

"It's all over now," she said. "You can come back in."

Eva was sleeping. She had shrunk and was thinner and whiter than ever before – while she was carrying the child we hadn't seen how terribly skinny she'd got, big and skinny, she looked as if she'd never wake up again. Lord, to whom shall we go?

The dead baby was lying at the foot of the bed.

"It's a boy," said mother.

He was as big as babies usually are when they start learning to walk and his eyes were closed as if he was asleep, he didn't seem to have suffered any pain but looked almost contented, he was so fat that his skin glistened and his fingers were spread because they were so fat and his cheeks were as round as if he'd got something big and tasty in his mouth, a sugar-loaf. And

Erik's Hannah explained to us what it was we could see: "He's eaten her away like a wild beast, he's eaten like someone with no limit to his stomach and then he's died, he's eaten himself to death, he's eaten and drunk until he had a stroke. He's sucked the life out of her."

And then after a while: "What kind of person would he have become?"

And finally: "Who might his father be?"

"That's a matter between Eva and our Lord," said mother.

But of course she was thinking: he's Karl Orsa's boy, he was like his father by nature, it was a mercy of our Lord to let him die, he was the kind that sucks life and blood.

But I'm sure she didn't think what I was thinking: Lord, why did you ever bother to create him?

After Erik's Hannah had gone mother and Johanna helped one another to wrap the baby in an old sheet, leaving his face uncovered, and they laid him on two floorboards that I brought in and set up between two chairs. And Eva slept so you could hardly see she was breathing.

"Now we have to get Karl Orsa over here," said mother. "He's got a right to see his child."

"It's evening," I said. "They'll have gone to bed at Karl Orsa's."

"Then we'll have to wake him up," mother said.

"He'll be in a pretty foul mood if he's not left in peace at night," I said.

"If you won't go I'll go myself," mother said.

So I went. It was dark at Karl Orsa's but I knocked on the door with a stone and the new servant-girl came out, the one who'd replaced Johanna, and I told her to fetch Karl Orsa.

"I wouldn't dare to," she said. "You'll have to do it yourself."

So I went up the stairs and opened his door and said: "Karl Orsa. Mother says you're to come over to our place."

And I thought now he'll kill me.

But he just got up immediately, he didn't say a word, not even to ask what it was mother wanted, he pulled on his trousers and his shirt and a knitted pullover and the dogskin coat that hung by the door and then he came, and he was in such a hurry that he almost pushed me over on the stairs, and when we got outside he half ran up the road, it had been snowing during the evening so it wasn't totally dark.

When we came in mother and Johanna were sitting by the table, they'd put Tilda to bed and Eva was asleep, she hadn't moved, and although the light was dim he saw the stillborn child straight away.

"That's your boy," mother said.

"So he never lived?" said Karl Orsa.

"He was already dead when her waters broke," mother said.

And he took the candle that was standing on the table and went up to the dead baby boy and leaned forward and shone the light on his face and stood there for quite a while saying nothing, and mother claimed afterwards that his eyes turned moist and he had to wipe his face with the back of his hand.

At last he said: "And he was big and handsome."

"He was too greedy, he ate himself to death in the womb," said mother.

"But a fine boy," said Karl Orsa.

"He was unnatural," said mother. "He almost sucked the life out of Eva through the navel-cord."

And then it was as if Karl Orsa remembered about her at last.

"She must be completely done in after this," he said.

"She's sleeping," said mother. "She's sleeping as if she never meant to wake up again."

"But she's got her zest for life," he said.

And he put the candle back on the table and stood where he was and seemed at a loss what to do, and mother sat examining her fingers, they were quite stiff now and there were small lumps on them and they nearly always ached. In the end she said: "What do you want us to do with him?"

And then I said, because I wanted to put an end to all this: "Stillborn babies are usually just buried. They don't need a funeral service."

"But he doesn't look like a stillborn baby," said mother. "He looks like a fully formed human being."

"I can take him," said Karl Orsa. "If I can do you that little service, Thea."

"You do as you wish," mother said. "It says in the Scriptures that the Lord shall turn the heart of the fathers to the children. So take your child, Karl Orsa. If anyone's got a right to it it's you."

And so Karl Orsa took the boy in his arms, he carried him as if he was an ordinary baby, and Johanna got up and opened the door for him so that he could get out, and what he did with him afterwards I don't know, we never asked; a stillborn child is like a stranger, not even Tilda asked about him the next morning.

Eva didn't wake up in the morning, and when Johanna lifted the rug we saw there was a lot of blood in the bed.

So I went straight over and fetched Erik's Hannah again.

"I had a feeling someone would be needing me," she said.

And when she'd examined Eva and looked at everything there was to see she said that that's how things were.

"The stillborn baby was too big," she said. "It's ripped her apart inside. It's torn the arteries in the womb. She'll soon have no blood left."

"So she won't pull through?" mother said.

"She might if the Lord performed a miracle with her," said Erik's Hannah.

Lord, you were with us all the time through all those days, why did you just look on, why didn't you stretch forth your omnipotent hand to help Eva? The eyes of the Lord are in every place, beholding the evil and the good, but why do you content yourself with beholding? Except for the times when you really turn everything upside down?

"So you don't know what to do?" said mother.

"If you've got any mustard," said Erik's Hannah, "you can rub it over her belly. But otherwise . . ."

"So there's nothing else?" said mother.

"No. Nothing else."

So I ran to the shop and got the mustard, and Johanna smeared it over her belly, and mother sat by the table and kept her eyes closed and didn't move, it was as if she was unconscious although she was sitting upright; when we spoke to her she didn't hear us, and Eva went on breathing, though slowly, until the afternoon, and then it was over.

She was eighteen years old.

When Johanna saw she was dead it was as if she herself was finished, she took Sabina and huddled up with her in our bed and turned towards the wall and lay quite still. But mother seemed to wake up, she opened her eyes and looked at me and said: "Now Karl Orsa has to be fetched."

"Do we really have to?" I said.

"We have to," she said.

So I went and got him.

I didn't say a word about how things were with Eva, but it was as if he knew it.

He went straight up to her bed, he didn't say anything, and he went down on his knees and lowered his head so that his face lay against her long hair, and how long he stayed like that I don't know, and now and then his whole body quivered as if someone had taken hold of him and lifted him up and shaken him, and mother sat quite still looking at him and saying nothing.

When he finally stood up his face was red and kind of swollen, and he didn't look at any of us.

In the doorway he turned round and said: "I'll take care of everything."

That was the only thing that was said. And however strange it may sound it was like a real help and comfort to hear it: that Karl Orsa would take care of everything.

[XIII]

And he really did take care of everything – he got a coffin and he took Eva to Norsjö; mother and I followed behind on a cart-load of oats. Johanna stayed at home with Tilda and Sabina, there were three horses in the funeral procession, the last of the loads was a pig's carcass and bundle of sheepskins that Karl Orsa was going to give to the parson and the church.

The parson spoke of thee, Lord, who hast mercy on whom thou wilt have mercy, and whom thou wilt thou hardenest.

Karl Orsa asked mother to travel beside him on the way back from Norsjö. It felt as if he was part of the house of mourning he said, and he told her he'd crossed off all our debts in the book now, he'd let us off everything, we were as free from debt as newborn babes.

But mother couldn't bring herself to thank him.

Mother never recovered after Eva's death. Her fingers got stiffer and stiffer and lumps appeared on her ankles and knees, but it was as if she didn't care about it. Johanna saw to the things that needed doing and Tilda was good at helping, so mother mostly sat at the table reading the Bible and when she thought she was alone she talked to herself.

In the New Year of '71 Karl Orsa came over and said that he wouldn't take any rent that year, we'd get a free year, he'd been thinking a lot about us, and we got the almanac anyway. As he was about to go he said: "Nobody plays the fiddle now, I suppose?"

"No," I said. "But I've thought of hanging it on the wall. It would be a sort of decoration."

But then Karl Orsa said he thought he had a buyer from Risliden, and when he left he took the fiddle under his arm, and Tilda started to cry because she seemed to think she'd inherit the fiddle, though she hadn't any talent for music.

In March I went to Baggböle and got a job there straight away, Lindström remembered me very well. During the summer I only went home for the haymaking, and when I finished in November I had enough money for the rent and more. Just before Christmas, on 17th December, Johanna had a girl; we christened her Eva after her aunt.

After Epiphany mother didn't get up.

"Why should I get up?" she said. "It's easier for me to lie here, and there's no point in wearing out clothes unnecessarily."

She was forty then, I was twenty-two, Tilda was seven, Sabina was one year old and had just learned to walk and Eva was newborn.

And mother couldn't stand music any longer. When Johanna sat down and played she said: "I get a pain behind my eyes from music. You can play when I'm asleep."

So Johanna played the harmonium in the evenings when mother had fallen asleep, though sometimes she woke up and said she was having such bad dreams and that it was probably because of the music, but she never told us what she'd dreamed.

Johanna worked hard, she looked after the byre and the little ones and mother and never complained. You know she never complained. She used to sing to herself, it was a sort of habit and she didn't know she was singing. "The splendour of the roses my heart to joy disposes, Whenever I stroll around the rose-garden fair."

I tried once to talk to mother about whether it might be an illness she had. But she just said that that's how things were, it might be some kind of weakness but nothing happens unless it's the will of the Lord.

But to this day I don't know who it was wanted her to die, whether it was herself or you, Lord.

She lived until the beginning of the summer. But on the second Sunday in June when we woke up she was dead. And I remember we sat down at the table when Johanna came in from the byre and I opened the Book and read the text for that day. Every branch in me that beareth not fruit he taketh away, and every branch that beareth fruit he purgeth it, that it may bring forth more fruit. Now ye are clean through the word which I have spoken unto you.

In the autumn, the day before I was due to leave for Baggböle, Karl Orsa came and said he'd decided to take care of Tilda.

"She's like an orphan now," he said. "And I'll never have any children of my own."

"Can I be in the shop, then?" said Tilda.

Sugar-loaves, she thought.

"She'd be like a foster-child," said Karl Orsa. "Not just living in."

"I think of her as a little sister," said Johanna.

But she probably said that mainly because she felt she had to, Tilda wasn't like either mother or Eva, she was most like Karl Orsa, she was calculating and shrewd and she had dark hair and brown eyes.

"I don't know," I said to Karl Orsa.

"This isn't a business matter," he said. "I'm not going to pay to take her."

"It's not that," I said. "I'm man enough to support my family, that I can tell you."

"It's only meant as a suggestion," said Karl Orsa. "An offer. That's all."

"She should be allowed to do what she wants herself," I said. "We shouldn't arrange things too much for children. We don't own their lives."

I was almost sure she would want to stay with Johanna, they were nearly always together and Johanna was amazingly patient with her.

"I want to be in the shop with Karl Orsa," she said.

And it made no difference that we tried to talk to her, she just looked straight ahead and didn't answer us, and she even went up to Karl Orsa as he stood by the wood-bin and took him by the hand, and it did look rather odd, he'd probably never held a small child by the hand before.

And she was in such a hurry that she didn't even want to take anything with her, not her clothes nor even the doll that I'd made the body and the head of and Johanna had sewn the clothes for – she was like an old person who's finally decided to start a new life, there was nothing at our place that she wanted to take along with her, she wanted to go at once and Karl Orsa said she could have the little room behind the kitchen all to herself.

Karl Orsa's Tilda. Everything must have a name.

So when I went to Baggböle there was only Johanna and Sabina and Eva left, and it felt emptiest of all because of mother.

[XIV]

Mother was not an ordinary person.

She seemed to tie her own life up with our lives so that she was inside us all the time, even if she wasn't anywhere near, it was as if she was beside us, and she still hasn't entirely faded away.

She always kept track of time like no one else, not that she always knew what time of day or what day it was, but in the sense that she was always aware of what had already happened and was done with for ever and what was taking place right now and what hadn't yet happened, things that were in the future and weren't to be worried about – she never talked about my father because he belonged to the past. Except towards the end, when she abandoned time altogether.

She said then that she would have liked to remember what he looked like, but she couldn't.

She had such a light and sunny nature. However many debts she incurred, her soul remained free of them all. She couldn't be affected within, there is nothing from without a man, that entering into him can defile him, but the things which come out of him, those are they that defile the man. When I was little and there wasn't enough food she would play the harmonium for us: "Lord! You graciously us spare Of your bounty each a share, Food and drink to us you give, That we all refreshed may live."

She was strong, she was stronger than Karl Orsa, he never really had any power over her.

[XV]

Karl Orsa's Tilda, when she was little she was my half-sister, but after she moved away from us we weren't related any more. In the autumn of '73 when Karl Orsa was fifty and Tilda was nine, she decided they should have a big party for Karl Orsa, the main customers and relatives from Granliden and Kvavisberg and Gallejaur, and she sent the farmhands over to us to fetch Johanna and the harmonium.

She herself wore a new frock from Skellefteå.

And she didn't know Johanna; she'd written on a piece of paper what tunes were to be played and she arranged that Johanna should be given beer and a chicken breast while the parson made his speech, and when the party was over she made sure that three crowns were paid for the music, but she said not a word to Johanna herself, she didn't know her.

For what man knoweth the things of a man?

I was at the sawmill at Baggböle for two years, I only went home for the haymaking and for a while in the middle of winter when they weren't sawing every day, and the earnings were enough for me to pay the rent and whatever Johanna had taken on credit while I was away.

A stacker should be able to carry three two-inch planks on his shoulder. On 20th November, '74, just before noon, I was carrying six two-inch planks on my shoulder – a man from Bratten called Alexi had carried five before me so the whole thing was his fault. Halfway up I had to move my left hand and my right foot slipped and something snapped in my back – the men behind me must have heard the crack though they say they didn't hear anything – something broke in my back just below the shoulder blades and I had to drop all six of the two-inch planks.

That's how things were.

And I couldn't lift my arms, they just hung there.

And I told Alexi from Bratten: "It's your fault. It was you who made me break my back."

So come New Year of '75 we had no money.

And Karl Orsa knew it.

"I'll settle up with Johanna," he said.

"You won't," I said. "Not as long as I live."

"You can play a piece for me, Johanna," he said.

And Johanna didn't have any choice, I went out and stood on the steps while she played, because I got a sort of pain in my chest from the music, it was so cold that I could see my hands turning white as I stood there, and I didn't go in until the harmonium stopped. But it was as if he didn't need anything more than the music on that particular day, he already had his dogskin coat on.

"Our Lord has said that we should be forbearing," he said as he left. "Though justice has to take its course."

And when he came again the next day he didn't ask for music. "Debt-recovery proceedings," he said. "If we can't settle up in a friendly manner. For those who do what the law demands shall be regarded as righteous. So there."

And the third time he just said he'd be going to Skellefteå the next day.

"If there was anything I could do," he said. "But the law is the law. And as you aren't willing to settle up in a friendly manner . . ."

Then I was completely at a loss and didn't know what to do;

in the evening I went to the byre. And there I sat talking to you, Lord.

"If I can't bring my questions to you I'm done for," I said.

And then I asked about everything.

When I came back in Johanna wasn't there, I could see right away how things were, there was nothing else she could do, and I told myself that when people have no choice they might do almost anything, and that was a kind of comfort.

When she came back she didn't say anything, we didn't talk about it that night, that's how things were, I followed her when she went to milk Taphath. Lord, to whom shall we go?

The following weekend he brought the almanac.

"And credit," he said. "If you need it you've got credit, Johnny. In case you run short of anything."

It seemed a matter of course to him, but to me it was a taunt, I didn't understand business. It felt as if he'd taken a billet of wood and smashed it in my face, and for a moment I couldn't see.

But then I stood up and went up to him, and he stepped out of the way as if he thought I'd do something to him, and I told him straight out: "Someone ought to kill you. If this thing in my back hadn't happened. If I could use my arms. Then I'd kill you."

And he looked at me, he didn't say anything, there was nothing to argue about, he could see I meant what I said. So he took his fur coat and left, he even forgot to put down the almanac.

And after that it was a long time before he dared to come to us again.

In June of '74 Johanna had a boy. He was called Alexis after my mother's father.

My back got better. But it was as if my head had got stuck, I couldn't turn my neck. And my arms improved so I could lift my hands up to my shoulders, I could carve wooden things with a knife and I could mend shoes, and when the woodcocks started calling I could carry my gun again. But I wasn't a stacker any longer, I wasn't any use to them at Baggböle nor at any other sawmill. So I couldn't earn anything any more.

But credit. We did have credit.

[XVI]

Right from the beginning and on to the end.

That's how things were.

When Job was in despair, when he sat among the ashes and had rent his mantle, he asked: "What is my strength, that I should hope? And what is mine end, that I should prolong my life? Is my strength the strength of stones? Or is my flesh of brass? Is not my help in me? And is wisdom driven quite from me?"

Finally I told Johanna that there was no mercy, we should try to help ourselves, for what did we have to lose? That too is a duty: to help oneself; what else could he take away from us?

Lord, what is the last mite?

She told me everything that used to happen when he claimed his dues, and it was as if she was cutting deep into me with a knife, but I knew I had to bear it, he always wanted it his own peculiar way, he was unnatural like that too, and it wasn't easy for Johanna to tell it all.

He'd said he'd come on Lady Day. I couldn't sleep that night.

When we heard his footsteps I went into the pantry and stood behind the door, I could see everything through the crack. Johanna sat down at the harmonium and I could see she was white in the face as if all her blood had run out.

But Karl Orsa didn't want music.

"Are the kids asleep?" he said. He looked his usual self, he looked like he did standing behind the counter in the shop.

And Johanna said what we'd agreed: "They're asleep. They're asleep and Johnny has taken the gun and gone to Fir Hill."

I had a knife in my hand, and I thought: if only you knew, Karl Orsa, that I'm standing here looking at you and that there's a knife in my hand . . .

"Eight crowns," he said to Johanna. "Eight crowns in the book." And: "No one can be burdened with debts for too long." And: "You're so pretty today. You blossom out more with every day that passes."

Then he went and lay down on the bed, and I thought Johanna looked like a sacrificial lamb, and I looked at the sheath-knife, it was grandfather's. But it had also been Jacob's knife. And then he undid his trousers and made himself ready, and he looked his usual self, he looked the same as he did when he was displaying a piece of cloth or a hammer handle in the shop, and Johanna climbed up and sat on top of him.

And I only waited a moment, just long enough for the blood that dimmed my eyes to drain away, and then I threw open the door and ran over to them, and Johanna jumped out of the way just as we'd agreed, and I cut hard and fast like when you cut a chicken's throat, and Karl Orsa never had time to realise what was happening.

All I got in my hand was the last half-inch of the head of his prick, it shrank like a snowball between my fingers.

I'd planned to tell him that from now on . . . But that just wasn't the way it went.

He sat up a little to see what I'd done, and Johanna stood behind me, a lot of blood was flowing and his prick wilted so there was almost nothing but skin left, and none of us said a word. I hadn't thought beyond that. I had no idea what would happen afterwards.

But nothing much happened at all. It wasn't only his prick that wilted, it was as if we were all slack and empty. He'll bleed to death, I thought. Never before had I seen a person bleed so terribly from a single part of his body.

Johanna came to at last, and she took up her apron from the stool in front of the harmonium and folded it and bound up Karl Orsa to stop the blood from flowing, and her hands were as careful and gentle as if she was swaddling a baby, but she didn't say anything. And Karl Orsa said not a single word, he lay quite still and it looked as if this was what he'd been expecting.

That it must have been intended.

He lay there like that until it was dusk outside.

Then he got up and dressed, and his face was as white and expressionless as if he was asleep, and then he left.

And the only thing that was said when he'd gone was what Johanna said: "What if he goes to Skellefteå? If he reports it?"

But I knew he'd never report it. How would he have explained it all?

That night, how I felt that night you alone know, Lord. It was like purgatory. I'd never before felt such guilt. And I thought, what if I'd killed him.

I don't know how Karl Orsa treated his wound. Whether he did it himself or had someone to help him. Maybe Tilda.

We didn't have credit any more. Three small children and no income and only one milch-cow and the hunting, I shot a stray reindeer at Ox Spring. You can't live more uncertainly than that. Only you, Lord, know how we managed.

At Midsummer Johanna earned five crowns from playing.

And one Sunday evening towards the end of summer, while I sat carving a cup for Alexis, Tilda came, Karl Orsa's Tilda, and she had only one message and she delivered it quickly, she didn't even come indoors: "Father sent me," she said. "He said I should tell you that if you need it and if you want to he's not unwilling. Regarding credit."

[XVII]

In the end that was our only way out. Credit. His credit was our salvation. Though we never said it, that without the credit . . .

Credit is like a pitcher that goes often to the well.

At Epiphany in '76 Karl Orsa turned up again, he was his usual self, it was as if what I'd done with the knife had never happened. He'd been thinking about the music all over Christmas he said, he had half a sugar-loaf for Sabina.

And Johanna played Christmas tunes for him.

And then he said: "Perhaps we could settle up, Johanna."

And that's when I saw red again, if only I'd been prepared but I wasn't, he was as strange and unnatural as the way of a serpent upon a rock, and I clenched my fist as if I'd been holding the knife.

But in the end I pulled myself together so that I could say to him: "My back's getting better with every day that passes. I'll soon be earning again."

"You won't be a man for several years yet, Johnny," he said. "And that's a fact."

Sabina was sitting on the bed with the sugar-loaf, Johanna looked at her, her face was all shiny from the sugar, and Johanna said: "I don't think I can bring myself to do it."

And then I said what I was sure would be the final word: "You can't manage it any longer, Karl Orsa," I said. "Not after the treatment I gave you. You're like a cripple from now on as far as that's concerned."

"I've thought about it," said Karl Orsa. "And I think it'll be all right. It feels as if it wouldn't be impossible."

And then none of us knew what to say, there seemed no way out, we were naked before each other. And before you, Lord.

Finally Karl Orsa got up and put on his fur coat, and in the doorway he said: "But you still play as beautifully as ever, Johanna."

He only said that because something had to be said, it wasn't really about the music, and Johanna never played as well as mother or Eva did.

When he'd gone Johanna said: "It's not because he wants to. It's only because of the debts."

"It's wickedness," I said. "Sheer wickedness."

And then she remembered a saying from the Bible: "He that doeth evil hath not seen God."

"Are you trying to excuse him?" I said.

"No one can excuse him," she said. "But he's still a human being."

I've thought a lot about that since then, and even now I don't understand what she meant: "But he's still a human being."

I should have asked what it meant, but that just wasn't the way it went. The fact that you're a human being isn't an excuse for anybody. Yet it's as if it meant that we're not guilty of anything. As if human beings are never really responsible for anything. As if human beings had paid a bit of their debt right from birth just by taking on themselves the burden of living a human life.

Perhaps that was what she thought.

If you had to think like that about anyone, then it would be Karl Orsa.

But Johanna never settled up with him again. The last debt we had in the shop was never paid off, and we no longer had any credit.

[XVIII]

In March when he was at the market in Skellefteå Karl Orsa discovered that people usually paid a deposit when they occupied a croft, it might even be written in law, and down south they always did.

"One hundred and sixty crowns," he said when he came back. "And anyone who doesn't pay his deposit can be evicted. That's what the law says."

"That's more money than I've ever seen in my whole life," I said.

"It's a tidy sum," he said. "But there's nothing I can do about it. We're all subject to the law."

And he went on: "You can't live the way you do, Johnny. A hand to mouth existence without order or method. It won't work in the long run."

"But what are you going to do with us?" said Johanna.

"I'm responsible for the place," he said. "That's the responsibility that's laid upon me."

And he also remembered a saying from the Bible: "As disorder and confusion lead to discord, so likewise doth order lead to peace."

"And Alexis?" said Johanna. "And Eva and Sabina? The little ones?"

"They aren't my children. Tilda's the only child I've got. I have the papers from the court. Tilda Markström. She's my only child."

"The children aren't guilty of any debts," said Johanna. "What would Our Lord say about that kind of order?"

And he thought hard for a moment, and then he said something that was totally incomprehensible: "Our Lord is order itself."

And after that there was nothing more that I or Johanna could say.

And the final thing he said was this: "The deposit has to be paid before midsummer. If not, you'll have to go. And the house."

Lord, the last mite doesn't exist. The last mite is the one that we can never pay.

[XIX]

Everything from the beginning to the end.

And that's what I wanted to ask you, Lord: had you decided all this from the beginning? Were we all bound in the bundle of life with you? If that was so, who among us could be guilty of debt? And if then we had no guilt, why did you use us as if we were responsible for everything?

That's all I want to ask you about.

Was it really true, as Karl Orsa said, that you, Lord, are order itself?

When Job had lost all he had to lose, he said: "And after my skin worms destroy this body."

Are we to be pure and free from debt only then, and not before?

We woke up early on Midsummer's Day, it was really still night, we were woken up by a hellish din and racket up on the roof, there was such a banging and clattering and thudding that we thought the roof was about to cave in on us, and Johanna wanted to take the children and get down to the cellar.

But I realised straight away what it was.

So I got up and put my clothes on and told Johanna just to lie still and not to worry because I was going to deal with this, there was a frightful noise up on the roof but it would soon be quiet again, and I took the gun, the one that originally belonged to Jacob, and the shot and powder and fuses.

And then I went out and no one saw me, I went right round

the house to the south side, and I got down behind the big rock that the children used to pretend was "home", and it was as if I thought: Now, at last!

It was Karl Orsa and two of his hands, they'd already broken off the guttering and lowest boards – it was grandfather who'd laid that roof long ago so it was well made – and on top of the ridge beam stood Karl Orsa, he had a big axe in his hand and it looked as if he was wondering whether he should tackle the chimneystack or the roof ridge itself, he wasn't used to hard labour and exerting himself. And I stared up at him and tried to make sense of him, it was as if I felt a sort of need to understand his thoughts. We aren't responsible for our thoughts, they rise up in us like weeds whether we want them to or not, thoughts are like writing inside us, they can't be separated from the life you've given us to live, you've filled the mind of every man, Lord, with special kinds of thoughts.

And I believe Karl Orsa thought he had no choice. He had been set to live that life and to sow his talents. And that's what he was doing as he stood there on the ridge beam holding the big axe in his hand, he was trading with the talents that had been entrusted to him, he was free of debt and guilt, it was the same for him as it was for Paul: he did not that which he desired, but that which he abhorred.

That's how things were and to whom shall we go?

So I loaded the gun and primed the fuse and cocked the hammer and rested the barrel against the rock, and I felt no guilt. I took careful aim, I've always been a good shot, and I took my time because I didn't know whether to aim at his head or chest or stomach, a stomach wound can be worse than any other, so I moved the stock very slightly up and down and thought: Now, Karl Orsa! And then, right then, just as I was trying to make up my mind like that, you Lord created this incredible thing that lies before me and beneath my feet, you intervened at last, it was just as if Karl

Orsa vanished from my sight, I couldn't see him any more with my aiming eye, and when I moved my head to one side and opened both eyes I saw the whole lot, the house and the foundations and the chimneystack and the ground the house stood on and the columbine that Johanna had planted in front of the porch, the whole lot moving and sort of sliding down the hillside the house was built on; the lower part of the slope had separated or split away from the rest of the ground and was slipping down the hill. And there was a roar as if the whole hill was about to collapse, and a cloud rose above the edge where the house had vanished so you couldn't see a thing, and I thought it isn't true but perhaps Karl Orsa finally got too heavy for the earth to bear.

And Johanna! And the littl'uns who hadn't yet lived their lives!

And a saying from the Bible came into my mind: And he that sat on the cloud thrust in his sickle on the earth, and the earth was cleaved – and I took out the fuse and laid down the gun.

But then it eventually went quiet and the smoke cleared and the dust, and I stood up and went over to this edge, here where I'm sitting now, and my legs were shaking so much that I didn't think I'd make it, and there was a sort of film over my eyes. But there was nothing to see below the edge, just the sandy soil and gravel and scree, not so much as a piece of board or a nail and no sign of life, and I couldn't think at all, everything that my thoughts had clung to all those years was swallowed up and buried and not even the chimneystack was sticking up, and even today, to this very day, I don't know which of us it was that you, Lord, thought justice should be done to, your kingdom is the sceptre of justice, whether it was me or Karl Orsa. Tilda seems to be his only heir.

Lord?

And though after my skin worms destroy this body, yet in my flesh shall I see God.

Peter Høeg

MISS SMILLA'S FEELING FOR SNOW

Translated from the Danish by F. David

"A subtle novel, yet direct, clever, wistful, unforgettable"
RUTH RENDELL, *Daily Telegraph*

"Smilla Jaspersen is a wonderfully unique creation of snow and warmth and irony. She shimmers with intelligence"
MARTIN CRUZ SMITH

Peter Høeg

BORDERLINERS

Translated from the Danish by Barbara Haveland

"It exerts the same chill grip on the imagination as its predecessor *Miss Smilla's Feeling for Snow*, posing questions and withholding answers with the same disconcerting skill . . . The power of the novel lies in the awesome truthfulness of the child's voice"   SALLY LAIRD, *Observer*

"The sustained intensity and brilliance with which the lives of these 'dark and dubious children' are captured is overpowering"   JOHN MELMOTH, *Sunday Times*

Boris Pasternak

DOCTOR ZHIVAGO

Translated from the Russian by
Max Hayward and Manya Harari

"The first work of genius to come out of Russia since the Revolution"
V. S. PRITCHETT

"A book that made a most profound impression upon me and the memory of which still does . . . not since Shakespeare has love been so fully, vividly, scrupulously and directly communicated . . . The novel is a total experience, not parts or aspects: of what other 20th-century work of the imagination could this be said?"

ISAIAH BERLIN, *Sunday Times*

Giuseppe Tomasi di Lampedusa

THE LEOPARD

Translated from the Italian by Archibald Colquhoun

"The poetry of Lampedusa's novel flows into the Sicilian countryside . . . a work of great artistry"

PETER ACKROYD, *The Times*

"Every once in a while, like certain golden moments of happiness, infinitely memorable, one stumbles on a book or writer, and the impact is like an indelible mark. Lampedusa's *The Leopard*, his only novel, and a masterpiece, is such a work"

BRUCE ARNOLD, *Independent*

James Buchan

HEART'S JOURNEY IN WINTER

Winner of the *Guardian* Fiction Prize

"I don't believe this country has a better writer to offer than James Buchan. I can't think of anyone who concedes so much of his own intelligence to his protagonists – doesn't mock or belittle them – and gives them so much world to do battle with" ***London Review of Books***

"Like Conrad, Buchan sews thrilling biographical jackets for his characters, made from threads of history"

JAMES WOOD, *Guardian*

Georges Perec

LIFE A USER'S MANUAL

Translated from the French by David Bellos

"A dazzling, crazy-quilt monument to the imagination"
PAUL AUSTER, ***New York Times Book Review***

"One of the great novels of the century"
GABRIEL JOSIPOVICI, ***Times Literary Supplement***

Aleksandr Solzhenitsyn

ONE DAY IN THE LIFE OF IVAN DENISOVICH

Translated from the Russian by H. T. Willetts

"A masterpiece in the great Russian tradition. There have been many literary sensations since Stalin died. *Doctor Zhivago* apart, few of them can stand up in their own right as works of art. *Ivan Denisovich* is different"

LEONARD SCHAPIRO, *New Statesman*

Eduardo Mendoza

THE YEAR OF THE FLOOD

Translated from the Spanish by Nick Caistor

"A magnificent short novel . . . a rural elegy and political fable and an adventure story all in one"

MICHAEL EAUDE, *Times Literary Supplement*

"All the characters and relationships are sharply and subtly drawn"

JOHN SPURLING, *Sunday Times*

To join the mailing list and for a full list of titles please write to

THE HARVILL PRESS
84 THORNHILL ROAD
LONDON N1 1RD, UK

enclosing a stamped-addressed envelope